FOREWORD

In this first volume of her trilogy about an East Yorkshire family, Ruth Braithwaite has attempted an imaginative reconstruction of the life of her grandmother, Martha Cousins, who was born on June 21st, 1849.

Martha spent many happy and interesting years in domestic service in Malton and then became the wife of Ben Smith, a successful businessman in Hull with a house in Kingston Square. Although some of her adventures are fictitious, the author has tried to paint a true picture of the world in which she lived.

The subject of the second volume of the trilogy is Martha's husband, Ben, who was the son of Sir William Worsley's woodcutter at Hovingham, the home of the present Duchess of Kent's family. Volume III, "The House in Kingston Square", deals with the fascinating life led by Martha and Ben in Hull - their trials and tribulations and their gradually increasing prosperity.

MARTHA
A Yorkshire Trilogy, Part 1

by Ruth Braithwaite

HUTTON PRESS

1983

Computer typeset by
Hutton Press Ltd.

Printed and bound by
B.A. Press
18 North Bar Within
Beverley, HU17 8AX

ISBN 0 907033 14 8

ACKNOWLEDGEMENTS

For the memories of the death of Mark Cousins at Cheesecake Farm and for information about his beautiful wife, Jane, the author is indebted to Mrs. Emily Grahame, of 68 Coldyhill Lane, Newby, Scarborough, whose mother, Mary-Hannah, was Martha's youngest sister.

For the photograph of Martha on her wedding day - featured on the cover of this book - she wishes to thank Mrs. Julie Cheeseman, of 112, New Village Road, Cottingham.

Above all she is indebted to the late Mrs. Elsie Cook, loyal and devoted servant of Martha and Ben Smith, who lived at Victoria Villas, Nafferton, in the East Riding of Yorkshire until she went to spend her last years with her daughter Mrs. Sylvia Watton, of Lodgers Green, Eastfield, Scarborough.

RB

CONTENTS

Page

ILLUSTRATIONS

Page

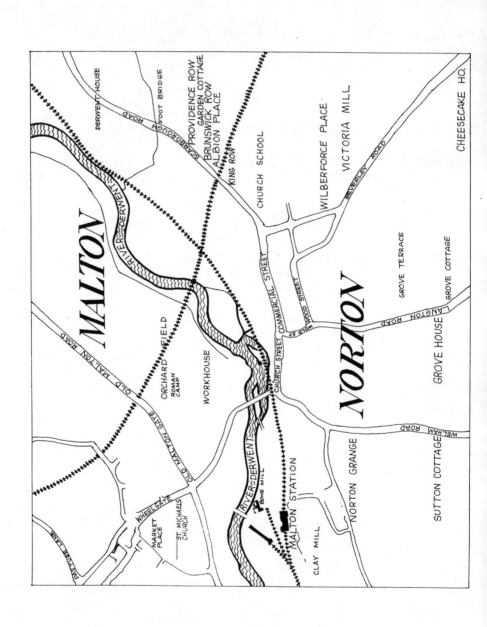

CHAPTER ONE: JUNE 21st, 1862. MARTHA COUSINS' THIRTEENTH BIRTHDAY.

Martha was not allowed even the luxury of tears on her birthday. "Dain't take on, there's a good lass - else the missus will be sending ye straight back 'ome. She'll think ye've got a fever hif ye go wi' your eyes all red."

Perhaps Aunt Lizzie's voice was not as harsh as her words. Martha clung to her for a long minute - as long as they could afford - and then she looked round at the wide-eyed little ones with the brilliant smile that made her suddenly pretty, and began to scold them as usual.

"Mind ye 'ave fire going, Liza, and git Thomas washed before yer mother's back. If Ah see ye on t'market day, Tilda, dain't let me see thee wi' 'oles in thi stockings or Ah wain't want to say you belong to me."

They knew she didn't mean this - and Tilly, who was the nearest in age to Martha and loved her more than her sisters, laughed as Martha meant her to. If Tilly had started to cry at that moment, Martha felt she would have had to give way and - what a disgrace if she had been sent home by the banker's wife at The Mount. "See you at Mart'mas." She turned her face away from the door.

Martha and her aunt were watched and commented on, loudly and pityingly, by their neighbours, who were all at their open doors on Providence Row. "She's only a lartle 'un, and pale as a ghost - some yal would've done 'er good." That was Maggie Bilson, who did not like the Ranters.

Martha's uncle, Robert Cousins, had been converted at a Camp Meeting when he was seventeen and had never touched "yal" since.

"Goodbye, Martha love. Dain't forgit us

11

will ye?" That salutation was harder to take
than some. Martha could not speak, but smiled
at the woman, her eyes shining unnaturally
bright.

"You've jist got ti think what a lucky lass
you be, Martha, love, getting a good place with
decent folks in a lovely 'ouse like that." The
Mount was one of the marvels of Old Malton since
it had been built by the banker at great expense
in the late fifties. "And in Malton too, better
than 'aving ti' go miles and miles away and
'appen being snowed hum at Mart'mas. Time'll
pass, ye'll see. Busier ye are, sooner it goes.
And dain't forgit ti say yer prayers ivvery
night, will ye, 'cos yer aunt and uncle wain't
forgit ye."

It might well be that, although The Mount
was only a mile and a half down the street from
Norton, when the green baize door of the
servants' quarters closed behind her, Martha
would be as irrevocably shut away from her
family and friends as any Carmelite nun. But
both of them clung to the hope that they might
see each other before Martinmas next year,
somehow. It might be that Mrs. Marney, the
Quaker banker's wife, would allow Martha to
attend class meetings at the house where the
Primitive Methodists met on Sundays - perhaps
once a month. At any rate her employer would
not expect her to attend Sunday evening service
at the Old Priory Church.

The fact that Martha came of a Ranter
family, that her hard-working uncle never got
drunk and her aunt dressed herself and her
daughters as plainly as Quakers, not allowing a
ribbon or a pair of curling tongs in the house,
had been in Martha's favour when her name was
suggested. Gertrude, the kitchen maid she was
replacing, had managed, in spite of long hours
and a strict housekeeper, to get herself

12

pregnant by a handsome gypsy tinker.

The Quakers were not noted for charity in such cases. Tales were current of the daughter of a Quaker family at Gilberdyke, a village near Hull, being walled in and left to starve to death.

But Mrs. Marney was a compassionate woman, and had made sure that the girl got safely home to her mother's cottage near Castle Howard. She had given her the wage due at Martinmas, much good advice and a letter for her mother, which would have to be read aloud to her by the vicar or the village schoolmaster as Gertrude had never been able to learn to read. But, although Mrs. Marney would remember her and the unborn child in her prayers, there could be no question of such a girl ever coming back to work in a respectable, Christian household.

Poor Gertrude would have run away with the tinker if he had not had a wife already. In the brief time they had had together, meeting in country lanes when she had been entrusted with an errand, she had fallen in love with him, and remained in love with him all her life. He was the fairy prince she was looking for every time she let someone else get her with child.

It had been deeply distressing for her mistress, whose care for the girl had, of course, been interpreted by some as certain proof that her eldest son Gavin was the father. A clever, sensitive young man of nineteen, Gavin had been more than a litle repelled by the slow-witted, bovine Gertrude, but he was always kind to his mother's servants. He had once taken Gertrude in the gig to market.

Mrs. Marney was pleased with what she knew of the Cousins family, and Martha did not seem like Gertrude in any way. Unlike her, she could read, write and cipher, and she did not speak in dialect when she was talking to her betters.

Besides, Martha's appearance at the age of thirteen was comically plain. Her dark hair could not be straighter or more tightly dragged back. If she had not happened to possess small, shell-like ears lying close to her head she would have looked even plainer.

Her eyes, however, were lovely - dark brown and full of intelligence, tenderness and humour - but when her prospective employer interviewed her they were dark with apprehension and cast down most of the time. The eyebrows were too strongly marked, and the lashes not particularly long. Her cheeks were always pale in winter. In summer her slightly olive skin had a golden glow. Her mouth was lovely, but too generously curved for fashionable beauty - not at all like the dainty cupid's bow of the Princess of Wales.

At thirteen, she was not fully grown, but her developing figure was sturdy and well-proportioned - a neat waist, a small, high bust, and a very straight back which she kept all her days. She had beautiful legs, and her shoulders and arms were so lovely that many years later, when Martha lived opposite Madame Clapham, the Court Dressmaker, Madame's niece Alice exclaimed once: "What a pity you don't wear evening dress! With your shoulders and arms you would look wonderful in a dress by my aunt." Alice was then engaged to Martha's son Ernest, a Methodist minister on probation.

The thought that one day she might live in Kingston Square in Hull would have seemed like a midsummer night's dream to the child-woman Martha on her thirteenth birthday, trudging along with Aunt Lizzie through the dust of the country lanes between Norton and The Mount at Old Malton, biting her lip and trying not to think how long it might be before she saw her own folk again.

She knew what Aunt Lizzie said was true:

14

she was very lucky to have got a good place. Her wage might only be a sovereign a year, her only day off at Martinmas - November 23rd - but she had the prospect of a roof over her head and enough to eat until she was an old woman, if she did not marry. It was a prize to be sought after by a parent or guardian, anxious for a young girl's welfare.

It so happened that Martha, dull with misery but immensely determined to do her best for her employer, was placed with a housekeeper who was prejudiced against Martha for two reasons. Firstly, Martha's relations were Ranters, and the housekeeper, Mrs. Barr, despised Ranters. Quakers were different: they were rich and respectable. The second and more powerful reason was that she had asked Mrs. Marney to see her niece Elizabeth, who had been kept at home until she was fourteen.

Mrs. Marney had consented to see Elizabeth, but she had also seen Martha Cousins, and she had chosen Martha. There was something Mrs. Marney liked about the girl - that quiet, dependable look even though she was so shy and nervous. "Those capable-looking hands - and she really does like looking after children. Her face quite lit up when I asked her about her brothers and sisters. I must have a girl who can help with the children."

The children had a nanny, but she was elderly, and recently her health had been giving cause for concern. Martha, maid-of-all-work, would have to help Nanny as well as Cook.

It was a very hot day in June. Martha and her aunt were thankful when they could walk in the shade of trees. They admired the lilacs and laburnums, they compared the progress of cabbages and beans in the cottage gardens, and inhaled the marvellous scent of roses whose names Martha would one day learn from the

15

gardener.

Now they were trudging along an uneven, rutted lane, where the trees were too far away to give them shade, but the hedgerows were lovely with their burden of pink and white may blossom scattered in careless profusion. They were hot and tired, and Martha's boots were dusty when they arrived at the double iron gates of The Mount.

The drive was well gravelled and wound upwards to the Big House, as they thought of it. It was a fine house with windows giving on to smooth green lawns with flower beds and shrubs. An old copper beech had been kept in the centre of the lawn, and in its leafy shade there were some elegant garden chairs and a table. This afternoon, Mrs. Marney and the children would have tea on the lawn.

The gardeners were at work, and they nodded at the sturdy-looking, pale-faced women in their dark, dusty clothes, and pointed without being asked to the flagged path that led to the back of the house, to the tradesmen's entrance and the servants' hall.

It was as pretty there as at the front, thought Martha. She liked it even better because there was an orchard. An ornamental iron gate in a high brick wall led to the kitchen garden and the greenhouses. A brilliant border of tall flowers - blue, purple, pink and white - could be glimpsed through the gate.

In these few tense seconds while they waited outside the white painted door with its panes of glass, a tiny, unfeathered, unlucky sparrow fell at their feet from its over-crowded nest in the eaves. Each woman recalled at that moment that last Sunday's preacher, a student on probation, had taken as his text "Not a sparrow falls", but, while exclaiming "Oh, the poor little thing!" they avoided each other's eyes.

16

Ranters they might be called, but if there were certain un-lettered old men in the congregation who loved to hear their own voices, the Methodist women were more noted for a quiet sensitivity and reserve.

Aunt Lizzie wiped the sweat from her face with the back of her hand as they stood and waited for someone to answer the bell. It had seemed almost an act of impertinence or folly to pull that bell rope.

A very clean, rosy-cheeked housemaid in a starched cap and with an apron over her long, black dress opened the door. Perhaps she had been expecting some masculine caller, for her bright smile vanished when she saw who it was. "Oh, it's the new maid, Martha, bain't it? Come in then."

They followed her down the tiled, clean passage and the maid knocked at the door of the housekeeper's room. "Mrs. Barr's ready for ye. Will ye go in."

Completely intimidated, they were shown into the room where Martha had been once before when she had been interviewed by Mrs. Marney herself, a being from another planet, a lady – but nevertheless she had had a soft voice and a smile for Martha.

The housekeeper's room seemed very grand to both of them, and the housekeeper, seated at her desk with her bunch of keys and her accounts in front of her, appeared a very stern woman.

There were bookshelves near the desk with several large leather-bound volumes: "Enquire Within on Everything", "Modern Domestic Cookery", the inevitable "Dr. Grahame's Domestic Medicine", and a family Bible.

There were two Windsor armchairs, a sofa, and a little footstool embroidered in Berlin wool which Martha admired. Even though it was such a hot day, a fire burned in the grate, which was adorned by well-polished fire-irons, a coal bucket, and a splendid copper kettle on a stand. A copper kettle like that was a status symbol, not for everyday use. It was awarded to a good servant when she had been seven years in her place. A family Bible was presented after ten years service.

Mrs. Barr did not ask them to sit down, but got up herself. Polite but unsmiling, she was only anxious to make sure that Martha had brought with her everything required. They opened the tin trunk with difficulty - it had been so well corded by her uncle the night before - and there, neatly folded, was the dark grey calico dress her aunt had made, and her three aprons and caps. In addition there was a darker dress for Sundays, the good worsted stockings Martha had knitted, three pairs of cotton drawers, two nightdresses and a chemise, two cotton petticoats and one flannel one, a black shawl, and the heavy linen napkins she would certainly need every month.

Aunt Lizzie had been thankful when Martha's periods began when she was only twelve. It was better for her chance of employment if a girl matured early rather than late, but there were times when she wished that this important female event could have been postponed until she was nearer leaving home. Menstruation was no easy matter to cope with in a two-roomed cottage, where every drop of water had to be brought from the well at the other end of Chapmans Row. Sooner or later one of the boys would find a bucket apparently filled with blood and ask questions. Little boys in those days were for ever being told that their sisters had had a nose-bleed.

"Why dain't she put yard key down 'er back, hif she's got a nose-bleed, mither?" young James would ask.

Well, at least the new girl was well provided for, thought Mrs. Barr, and it was as well that she hadn't worn the grey calico for walking from Norton. She would have got it dusty already on such a day, and she looked so hot and perspiring. What a sallow skin she had! Mrs. Barr thought of her prettier niece and sighed, but she was not a heartless woman, and before she took Martha upstairs she spoke kindly to her aunt.

"She'll come to no harm here, Mrs. Cousins. If she does her work well she'll never go short of nothink. Dain't ye worry about her now. She's come to a God-fearing house, ye must remember that."

"Ay, Ah knows that, Mrs. Barr. Ah'm thankful ti God for it. She's a good girl, our Martha is."

Aunt Lizzie, having assured the housekeeper that Martha was the strongest of the family and never knew what it was to be ill "though she nivver 'ad mich colour" gave her niece a kiss that was almost perfunctory, because how could it be otherwise, here in this house of strangers? Then she went back alone down the tiled passage and out into the sunshine. Tears blinded her now, and she could let them fall at last.

All Martha longed for in her own mental agony of homesickness and insecurity was to get to work at once. If they would give her some hard work to do she would show them that it was true what her aunt had told Mrs. Barr: she was a strong girl and a good worker.

"She's sturdy enough, and well-mannered, but I've got the training of her to start on," thought Mrs. Barr as she went ahead of Martha upstairs, up more stairs, up still more stairs, with Martha following, sweating more and more as the tin trunk, corded again, grew heavier.

At last they reached the landing with the
housekeeper's room and the maids bedrooms.
Martha had a garret under the roof all to
herself. She looked with horror at the bed she
would sleep in - it was big enough for three or
four of them at home. Surely, surely she
wouldn't have to sleep by herself?

The mattress was spotless, so were the
twill sheets and pillowslips and the two
blankets and the counterpane, all folded on a
chair waiting for her to make up the bed. There
was a table with a bowl and a jug, and even a
rickety chair and a small mirror on the wall.
The window was quite large and overlooked the
orchard and the kitchen garden. All the rooms
in that house, even in the servants' quarters,
were light and airy - and, of course, intensely
cold in winter.

What drew her eyes was a huge iron bell
hanging in a corner of the room near the bed.
It was explained to her that she would be the
very first in the household to be roused by that
bell, which was connected with the housekeeper's
bedroom. She must get up immediately, go down
and light the kitchen fire and clean all the
grates and lay the fires. Coal was brought in
last thing at night by a manservant.

When she had blackleaded the kitchen stove
and swept the hearths and polished the coal
buckets and fire irons, the kitchen fire would
have supplied hot water. She must wash herself,
put on a clean apron and take hot water to the
other servants - to Mrs. Barr first, of course.

If there were many things that were new and
bewildering, there were simple tasks which she
had always taken a pride in doing well. Martha
had a sense of beauty and order which had always
made her rejoice at the sight of a clean hearth,
and a kitchen range that was blackleaded to a
satin smoothness, with the brass knobs, fender

and fire irons shining as brightly as the flames leaping up the chimney.

Gertrude had always been slow, though a good enough worker when it came to scrubbing out cupboards or washing the passage. But Martha did not need to be told what needed to be tidied or reminded to put things back in place exactly as before. She did not have to be reminded to wash her hands before preparing vegetables. She might not have a fresh complexion and fair hair like Alice the housemaid, but "she bain't frittened o' soap 'n water," Cook remarked to Mrs. Barr.

Martha envied her employers only one of the many luxuries they enjoyed in that fine house - the hot water which they had in such abundance. It was wonderful to have running water, to turn a tap and watch the water cascade miraculously into the sink. Oh, those buckets and bowls which had to be filled from the well at the other end of Chapmans Row, and then had to be guarded from careless little ones who would spill the precious water. As well as two sinks, the kitchen and the scullery, the Marneys had a bathroom for the family, and a water closet.

They even had sitz baths in their bedroom as well as the jug and bowl on the wash-stand, and there were actually two earth closets in the garden for the servants. These were separated by a partition, not just two holes next to each other.

Cook, who like Nanny had been with the family for a long time, used to talk about the facilities for servants in her first place, somewhere on the Wolds: "A bucket and a pair o' tongs, that was all we had."

Tired as she was, for Martha her moment of bliss came that evening when she was taken up to the nursery. There were eight young Marneys. Gavin, who was nineteen, was working in a publisher's office in London. He had broken with family tradition by refusing to go into the bank. Henry, seventeen, good-looking, and popular with everyone, was already a clerk in his father's bank in Malton. Martin and Emma were fifteen-year-old twins. Martin was away at boarding school in York.

When Martha went into the nursery, Nanny had the baby, Rachel, in her arms, a delicate-looking, fair-haired infant with enormous blue eyes. Eleven-year-old Master Reginald, dark-haired like his mother, was an attractive but rather arrogant boy. He was sitting at a table playing Halma with Sarah, an eight-year-old with long, fair hair and a lovely face. They paused to say "Good evening, Martha" politely when Nanny introduced the new maid, and after a moment's appraisal went on with their game - Master Reginald was winning, as usual.

Three-year-old Edgar was sitting on the rug at Nanny's feet, playing with a pile of lettered bricks. He had his mother's dark hair and blue eyes with long lashes. They were a good-looking family, Martha thought. Fancy children being so fresh and clean at the end of the day - and yet it seemed they were all going to have a bath before they went to bed.

Martha was thrilled when Nanny asked her to hold the little one. The baby's eyes focussed on the stranger's dark, sallow face and seemed as fascinated by Martha as Martha was by the baby. Watching her with Rachel, Martha's firm, brown hand supporting the child's head, Nanny saw at once that she was used to handling babies carefully.

Nanny was preparing to bath the baby. "When we've seen to baby, you can see to the other bairns, can't ye? Ye see, love, me heart starts thumping when I try to do too much."

Nanny's voice was regretful and

matter-of-fact, not self-pitying. She was
blue-lipped; she had had asthma all her life,
and it was amazing that her physical heart had
not given up years ago.

She was the architypal Nanny. Martha felt
sympathetic towards the old woman, and yet
strangely puzzled and even repelled. She also
possessed a strong maternal drive. She knew
instinctively that Nanny wanted nothing more
from life than what she got - to devote herself
to the care of "the bairns" - and yet it wasn't
right. There was something profoundly unnatural
and wrong that such a woman should be a
life-long substitute for the real mother.

Poor Nanny, with her long, rather
melancholy, kind horse-face, her enormous
sagging bosom, large stomach and great spreading
hips beneath her neat uniform had somehow been
dehumanised, degraded, made animal-like by this
long self-sacrifice. Like a beast, she was
valued by human beings only for her usefulness
to them.

Nanny would never be cast off by the family
even if she became too ill to do any more for
them. She knew that she would not end up in the
workhouse, and she was grateful for that every
day her infirmity increased. Even if Mrs.
Marney had not been a woman who cared about her
servants, the children to whom she had been a
surrogate mother loved her too much to allow
poor Nanny to become destitute.

Still, it was too much to expect that if
she became bed-ridden she could be nursed in her
employer's home for long. Careful enquiries had
been made about her relatives, who had seen very
little of Ada Lumley since she went into service
as a nursery-maid when she was thirteen.

There was a widowed sister at Hovingham who
would be able to care for her, with the help of
Nanny's pension. Mrs. Marney would pay her

five shillings a week when she had to leave their service. So Nanny, she was thankful to say, had no financial anxieties. Her sister had been to see her and was greatly impressed with what she heard of how much Ada had managed to save. On Mr. Marney's advice she had bought War Loan certificates with her savings, and the pension of five shillings as well seemed almost too good to be true.

But Nanny secretly hoped that she would be able to go on living at The Mount until she died. When she had left home her sister Deborah had been a child of three. This thin-lipped widow was a stranger, and she did not want to die in a stranger's house.

So Martha was going to bath the other three children in the nursery when Nanny had put baby in her cot. Martha, still not grown to her full height, flushed suddenly as she caught the curious, rather arrogant eye of Master Reginald. Surely, surely Nanny couldn't expect her to bath a boy of eleven!

The children had their bath in front of the fire in the nursery, although of course it would have been easier for the servants if they had been allowed to use the bathroom. Martha had to empty the bath after baby had had her bath. Master Reginald always had the first bath in the new clean water - somehow that had become his prerogative - and then Edgar was bathed, and sometimes Sarah shared his bath.

Reginald watched the bath being re-filled and frowned: "I'm not going to let her bath me!" Nanny was too ill and tired to argue. That was one reason why Master Reginald was the spoilt one. To Nanny, all the children, even Gavin and Henry, and Martin and Emma who were allowed to use the bathroom were still her babies. Master Reginald must get used to the new nursemaid. Just as he was really only an

24

infant, so Martha, the new maid, in spite of not
being very tall, was a servant, whose feelings
no-one would have dreamed of considering.

Whatever Master Reginald thought, Martha
knew there was no escape for either of them.
Nanny was dozing a little in her rocking chair.
She simply said: "Nonsense, Master Reginald.
Get ready now, do." But clearly she was no
disciplinarian in her present state.

Martha's embarrassment faded as she
realised how much Nanny depended on her. "After
all, I am thirteen," she said to herself, her
lips tightening. In her world that was the age
when childhood ended and one had to take on
adult responsibilities.

She looked round: "Here you are, Master
Reginald. There's the bath towel, here's the
soap and the sponge. Now do you want me to
scrub your back with the loofah?"

She was as bossy as she could be at home
when occasion demanded. She knew she could not
trust Master Reginald any more than any other
boy to get clean in the bath without some
supervision. She had got to make sure that he
was clean from his neck to his heels before he
got out. She didn't want dirty marks on the
towels.

"Did you get that climbing a tree?"

"How did you know?"

"Boys always get bruises like that climbing
trees - unless they've been fighting."

"There's nobody to fight with."

Master Reginald was not allowed to play
with the village boys. He was hoping to go away
to boarding school soon like Martin.

Ten minutes later, Master Reginald emerged
clean but sulky. The new maid was a tartar and
no mistake. He didn't think he was going to
like Martha.

Strong as she was, when the time came to

carry the tall brass jug of hot water upstairs
to her own narrow room under the eaves, Martha
was so tired that for a few seconds she sat on
the bed wishing she could just curl up and go to
sleep. Dazed with fatigue, she pulled her
clothes off, carefully undoing buttons and
untying tapes because she would have no time to
waste in the morning.

Naked, she stood and washed herself all
over as she had been longing to do all day. She
hung her clothes on the rickety chair by the
window. It was midsummer night, her birthday
night. For a few seconds she gazed at the back
garden and the orchard which she had last seen
in the morning sunshine with Aunt Lizzie. It
was even more beautiful now, by moonlight.

They would all be asleep at the cottage by
now. Maybe if she had been at home, sharing a
bed with two of her cousins, she would have been
too hot to sleep. She might have been standing
at the window as she was now, gazing at the
stars and hoping she would dream of a handsome
young man, the lover whose face a girl was
supposed to see on midsummer night.

Freshened by the stand-up bath and the cool
night air, she unpacked one of her cotton
nightdresses. She must unpack her other clothes
in the morning, somehow, but now she must make
her bed before she could lie in it. After all,
she wasn't frightened of sleeping alone. On
such a night as this, it was a luxury to be able
to stretch between cool sheets, to have a pillow
that hadn't to be shared.

If Martha dreamed, that midsummer night, of
the man she was going to marry, the crash of
that great iron bell over her head made sure she
had no time to remember what he was like. Her
dreams fled like mice before a sudden shaft of
light.

He might be dark or fair, rich or poor,

plain as Uncle Robert, or handsome as her father, Mark Cousins, had been. She only knew she must hurry into her clothes and go down to light the fire.

Martha had loved her father more than anyone else in the world: after five years his memory was as fresh in her mind as the scent of flowers a blessed breeze from the east was bringing into her room as she dressed. But it was another scent, totally dissimilar, a sharp, acrid, winter smell of burning wood that sometimes brought his face before her. A smell which others might find piquant would for Martha always be the smell of death.

CHAPTER TWO: CHEESECAKE FARM.

Martha saw her father's armchair with its high, winged back, covered in red Morocco leather, placed on top of the bonfire. Surely it was a nightmare she was having, a bad dream about November the Fifth, when they were at Weaverthorpe...

She half expected her brothers to put an effigy of Guy Fawkes in the chair before they set it alight - her father's favourite chair, the chair he sat in when he changed into his plum-coloured velvet jacket, as he always did at the end of the day. Martha had so often found a refuge there in his arms.

The bonfire was lit now. Her eldest brother, Mark, was standing beside her, an arm protectively round her shoulders, as the flames leaped higher.

"Why are they burning our home, Martha?" That was little Mary-Hannah, who was only three, clinging to Martha's hand. She at least was fully aware that what was happening was real, and she was asking the eternal child's question - "Why?"

"Because father died of the smallpox." Martha, half choked with tears she must swallow, could add no more.

Mary-Hannah's great dark eyes, wide open with wonderment, never left the bonfire. Looking down at her face, the beauty of the child's soft skin made incredibly lovely by the glow of the fire, Martha was reminded again of last Guy Fawkes night at Weaverthorpe, how the faces of the villagers crowding round the bonfire had reminded her of the faces in an old oil painting that hung in their hall.

At least none of the pictures had to be destroyed - only the furniture her father had touched, the desk he used, the chairs he sat in, the bed in which he had died.

Mark Cousins had only just bought Cheesecake Farm at Norton, which is divided from the town of Malton by the River Derwent, when he died of smallpox. There were four boys, the eldest, Mark, was seventeen and well able, his father knew, to manage the farm if need be – but not experienced enough to take his father's place when he went to the cattle auction at Malton or the horse sales at York.

His son was a good worker, he was strong, and he had a good head on him, like all the Cousins, but he was inclined to be shy. Although he was clever enough in his own way, he was not quick-witted: he lacked the confidence for knowing when to bid and when not to bid. When buying and selling, one needed to know more about men as well as beasts than could be learned in seventeen years.

His father had put off selling old Bess, although she was not much good now except for giving the children rides. Their mother, who was as unsentimental about animals as she was about children, complained about being driven in the gig by Bess.

She must go, Mark decided now. His mother must have a smart grey, if he could afford it, so that she would be treated with proper respect and not given pitying glances when she drove into Malton. A beautiful widow, a woman who would always look at least ten years younger than her age – which was not too common in those days – Jane was a beauty all her life, though she lived to be eighty-six.

One of his father's friends, James Jemison, was a horse dealer. He was a widower who had lost his wife and little girl twenty years ago during an epidemic of typhoid. He had a reputation for fair dealing, and Mark was grateful for his company at the horse sale, but

29

he was amazed when Jemison, having bought a grey
at a price Mark could not afford, sold it to him
at half the price he had given.

They had been neighbours when the Cousins
family lived at Weaverthorpe. Mark knew that
Jemison was a generous man who liked to give his
friends hospitality, but "Nobody could get the
better of James Jemison at a deal," their father
had said.

Mark asked his mother if Jemison could come
to their home for supper, half expecting a sharp
refusal. She hesitated, and then agreed.

Jemison came, in his best Sunday suit with
manners to match, thought Mark, listening to him
praising their mother for cook's light hand with
pastry, for the beautiful home she had made at
the centuries old farmhouse, which had got its
name from a legend that pilgrims passing that
way were always given a piece of cheesecake
there.

The Chippendale chairs round the polished
dark table had one carver missing - the one
their father had sat in at the head of the
table. There was some fine silver, and there
were glowing oriental rugs, one of them thrown
over a chest in the Continental custom - but
Jemison knew that the Cousins had Flemish blood.

Jane's black silk dress was trimmed with
Brussels lace. When tears came into her dark
eyes, she dabbed at them with a lace-trimmed
handkerchief. Her skin was as creamy as the
lace, he thought. She was not the kind of
farmer's wife who went out in the fields to take
bread and cheese and cider to the men.

She was a lady and she was beautiful, but
he was not in love with her. He knew that she
looked down on him because he was not a
gentleman. It was a matter of condescension
that she had invited a horse dealer to her
table, at Mark's request.

A farmer's wife who did not lift a finger was a liability unless she was the wife of a gentleman farmer with thousands of acres, and Cheesecake Farm was nothing like that size. It was only three hundred acres, but the farmhouse was good, and the farm buildings and the stables were in good order. There was room for a dairy herd and some fields of wheat and barley as well as sheep. And it was what Jemison wanted more than anything, land.

Jane had brought out the Damson gin made two years before during a particularly good summer. Even Wesleyans had home-made wine and gin, as well as ale. Jemison knew it was more potent than anything the landlord sold at The Green Man in Malton.

Not too many men would want a widow, however, beautiful, who had seven children, but he could not feel as if he were doing her a favour, while she poured tea out of that silver tea-pot. He felt that he would be glad of a sip of the Damson gin too. "I needed some Damson gin to give me Dutch courage," he said to himself - the kind of thing he might say aloud some day to his men friends. He really preferred the company of men, and he preferred talking about horses to talking about women.

On his second visit to Cheesecake Farm, when he proposed marriage, James Jemison treated Jane almost as directly as he did a prospective buyer when he was selling a horse.

"I had a great regard for your husband. Mark was a fine man, and I'm not fit to clean his boots, I know that, but I'm not a poor man, I've made a lot of money over the years, and I've had no-one to spend it on since Lucy died. I could help young Mark and the boys make a go of Cheesecake Farm if I was here. We would have to get married, d'ye see. If I lived here as farm manager tongues would wag. I know ye can't

love me as a husband, that doesn't matter. I've
lived long enough without a wife not to bother
about things like that (and there's always the
barmaid at The Mitre)."

"Ye can sleep i' the best bedroom and I'll
take one of the others - there's plenty of room.
I reckon we're alike in one way, Jane. We've
both loved and lost and 'tis all in the past,
but I hope ye can abide having me about the
place. Ye see, me dear, it's like this: You've
got the farm, and I've got the know-how."

Perhaps it was a marriage of convenience:
she had no children by Jemison, but he replaced
the furniture which had been burnt and bought
her silk dresses. Even when times were hard,
after a bad harvest, nothing was ever allowed to
disturb Jane's peace of mind.

The children, of course, were not
consulted. The idea of his mother marrying the
horse dealer was too much for young Mark. He
felt as if Jemison had made a fool of him,
selling him a horse cheaply in order to make
love to his mother. He quarrelled with his
step-father and went to farm in Canada, never
returning to England. James Jemison had taught
him one thing of value, he said: never to trust
a horse dealer.

If their mother was pleased to have the
smart grey to draw her gig instead of poor old
Bess, the children, especially the girls, were
almost as heartbroken to lose their pet as they
had been at the death of their father. Bess
belonged to the happy past, before the bonfire.

To Martha and Annie, the two older girls,
aged eight and fourteen, James Jemison seemed
every bit as wicked and despicable as their
brother Mark said he was. The youngest, Mary-
Hannah, who was more often with her mother, saw
a different side of her step-father. Jemison
was fond of children and spoiled her,

remembering the little girl he had lost with his first wife, Lucy.

He was appalled to find how many maids Jane had in the kitchen. It was ridiculous to bring up her daughters to do nothing, he said. Two of the maids were dismissed, and Martha and Annie were given some of the housework. Jane was not used to unskilled service. There were so many altercations between their imperious mother and the rebellious daughters that life was impossible. Jemison agreed to get maids for Jane, but he refused to keep all her daughters in idleness until they married.

Martha had never been close to her mother. As a little girl, she had been a tomboy who loved climbing trees with her brothers and the village children. Jane would reach for her vinaigrette and smelling salts when she appeared with a torn dress or spoke in the Yorkshire dialect she had heard in the street. "The sight of that child brings on my migraine," she said once.

When their father died and the furniture had to be burned because of the smallpox, when their mother knew that the two older girls would have to go into service, she seemed to lose all affection for them, as if they were already members of a lower caste with whom she could not be expected to be on intimate terms.

Annie was good with her needle. She would leave home to be a lady's maid, and Martha was packed off to Aunt Lizzie Cousins.

Although she did not know it then, Martha would soon lose touch almost completely with her family. Aunt Lizzie and Uncle Robert were Primitive Methodists, or Ranters. Mark Cousins and his family had attended the Wesleyan chapel at Weaverthorpe, the village where Martha was born. After her marriage to Jemison, Jane ended her connection with the Methodists and attended church.

Nobody had prepared Martha for her adoption. She had been mystified by the number of cases her sister Annie was packing for her when she was only going to stay at Aunt Lizzie's for a week or two, as she supposed. Her summer clothes as well as her winter ones - her best boots and her little fur-trimmed velvet pelisse - she would never be able to wear that at Aunt Lizzie's.

"You never know what the weather's going to be like, from one day to another," Annie had replied when Martha told her she was packing too many things.

As well as Martha's entire wardrobe, Aunt Lizzie was handed five sovereigns in a sealed envelope by Martha's brother John, who took her and the cases in the gig, his sister little dreaming as she sat beside him that she would never go to Cheesecake Farm again until she was a married woman with a child of her own. Martha would go into service when she was thirteen, but she was still only eight years old - the five sovereigns were to pay Aunt Lizzie for her keep.

It was a pity that the cottage was so small, with so large a family, but Martha had not minded sleeping with her cousin Tilly and one of the little ones when she had stayed there before.

Martha and Tilly were nearly of an age. They had always got on well, and it was remarkable how seldom young Liza, who shared their bed, had what she called "an accident". None of the young Cousins suffered from nightmares or bedwetting, but of course there was always a babe in arms and another just able to walk, so Tilly and Martha were used to getting up early and going to the well to bring back buckets of water, slung on a haul across their shoulders like milkmaids.

It was fun at first, but there were frosty
mornings when both girls had tears in their eyes
as they held their frozen fingers close to the
fire until life came back into them, with so
much agony.

Martha had never quarrelled with Tilly
until the day she went up to their bedroom and
found Tilly trying on one of her best dresses,
preening herself in the small, cracked mirror.

"That's mine, Tilly ... and it doesn't
suit you. You can't wear a dress like that -
not with those boots - and your hands all red
raw. It shouldn't have come here. It's for
when I go home."

Tilly stared at her cousin, wide-eyed, even
more amazed than Martha had been when she saw
her wearing her best dress. "Dain't ye know why
they brought all them cases? Ye bain't going
back to Cheesecake Farm, no, never, Martha,
you've come to stay with us till ye go out to
service."

Martha knew Tilly wasn't lying. She
remembered Annie telling her they would both
have to leave home and go into service, because
their step-father had said he could not keep so
many of them at the farm. She understood now
why Annie had packed all her clothes. "But they
could have told me, they could have told me."

She did not say this aloud, but the blood
rushed into her cheeks and her eyes flashed.
She was furious with Annie. All the time her
sister was packing her trunks she had been
asking "Why am I taking this? and this?"
Couldn't they have told her the truth and spared
her such humiliation?

Tilly saw the anger flare in Martha's face,
and thought it was directed at her. Tears came
into her eyes as she began to undo the little
pearl buttons on the sleeves of the grey silk
dress.

35

"Dain't get in a stew, Martha. It bain't my fault.... I didn't think ye'd mind hif I tried it on. It's so soft and nice. It's silk, bain't it? Did yer sister Annie make it?"

Silently, Martha took the dress from Tilly, folded it, and knelt to put it away in the trunk. When she stood up, she gave the corded trunk a tremendous kick with one of her sturdy, scuffed boots. Then she sat on the bed and tears began to stream down her cheeks - everything around her was blotted out for Martha. Tilly had never seen anyone so big cry like that, almost silently, but totally abandoned, as drowned in her tears as any child.

Very much alarmed, Tilly ran downstairs for her mother.

It was lucky that Aunt Lizzie had a heart big enough for all her children, and for Martha as well. A maternal instinct and a large family by no means go together. Aunt Lizzie was known in the village as a remarkable woman, because she succeeded in rearing every one of her fourteen children. They were ill sometimes, but they always seemed to escape the major epidemics of typhoid, diphtheria and smallpox which decimated other families.

When they were ill, Aunt Lizzie would leave her husband's bed, wrap the child in blankets and make up a bed for it on the rag rug in front of the fire. She made sure there were no draughts. Sausages made of old stockings stuffed with rags were put under the door and along window sills. The bright-eyed, feverish child was soothed with blackcurrant tea and kindness - Aunt Lizzie did not believe in laudenum, although most mothers swore by it for a restless child. While she sat in her rocking chair, the child lay watching the glow of the fire reflected in the brass knobs of the fender and usually fell into a deep, refreshing sleep towards dawn.

Although Martha was not physically ill, her suffering being confined to the heart and mind, Aunt Lizzie made up a bed on the floor for Tilly and Liza that night, and she slept in Martha's bed, holding her in her arms and letting her sob out her trouble. "They didn't even say goodbye .." Martha repeated over and over again, until at last she was too tired to do anything but listen to Aunt Lizzie's soothing words.

Martha knew in her heart that her mother had not loved her, but, even when a mother is neglectful, uncaring, even cruel, a child's heart mysteriously, illogically - as if the child must worship some ideal mother - always, whatever the mother has done, bears unshakeable loyalty to the one who gave it life.

Perhaps Aunt Lizzie with her instinctive wisdom knew this. "Ye mustn't blame thi mother, love. She's had so much to go through, ye see, losing your father, and knowing you and Annie was going into service she thought it might be better for ye to be with us, so ye could get used to helping me a bit. And ye are a good help, Martha love. I dain't know how I managed without ye, I dain't. And then, love, when ye go hinto service, hif you're lucky, why, ye might get a place as a nursery maid and get to be a Nanny. Ye love bairns, dain't ye, Martha?"

Although she did love children, Martha did not grieve for her young sister, Mary-Hannah. Mary-Hannah was a dainty little thing, with her mother's beauty. One daughter was a precious commodity, everyone needed a daughter for their old age. The only girl at home, and the youngest, would be sure to be spoilt. Mary-Hannah had always been her mother's favourite.

But even little Mary-Hannah had been lifted up to see her father lying in the coffin with

37

the glass lid, made according to the custom of the Huguenots - a sight she remembered all too vividly for the rest of her life.

CHAPTER THREE: MR. MARNEY.

After all, she had slept much better than if she had been at home, in Aunt Lizzie's cottage which was so stuffy in summer. The sun was shining, and she could hear the birds singing. They sounded very near, because she was so high up.

Compared to her feelings on the morning of her birthday, she felt almost light-hearted. A measure of self-confidence had replaced the agony of nervous apprehension. Today, at least, she would go into a kitchen which was no longer strange.

But, after all, there was something she had not expected which disturbed her that morning. Going into the master's study to clear the grate - Mr. Marney had a fire even on summer evenings - Martha was startled by the sight of a heap of gold coins scattered on the marble mantelpiece, and there was a silver florin in the big leather armchair near the fire.

Of course she had been warned by her aunt, as most girls going into service were warned, to be careful when taking up a carpet or rug. It was a favourite trick of employers to test a new maid's honesty by leaving a small coin underneath, but she had never thought she would see so much money left about so carelessly.

It worried her very much all the time she was cleaning the grate and polishing the fire irons. The clock on the mantelpiece ticked steadily on, but that was the only voice in the room. It could give her no advice about what to do. When it had ticked away for ten minutes and her work was done, she was very thankful it was time for her to get herself washed. The kitchen fire had soon heated the boiler. She wanted to tell Mrs. Barr about that money lying on the mantelpiece in the study.

The housekeeper was sitting up in bed in

her high-necked cream cotton nightdress, her long, dark hair brushed and ready to put up. If she had been timing the new maid, she had no cause for complaint. Martha was early, but she could not know until she got down how well she had cleared the hearths or how bright the fire irons were.

"Good morning, Martha. Is that water really hot? Put it over there."

"Please, ma'am."

"Well, Martha, what is it?"

"Please, ma'am, there's a lot of money on the mantelpiece in the master's study, and a florin on the chair. I put the florin with the other money."

"Oh, that'll be Mr. Marney. He sometimes puts his change on the mantelpiece and forgets it. Did ye count it?"

"No, ma'am, I didn't. I thought I'd better ask you what to do."

"You haven't dusted the mantelpiece, then. You'd best go and count it and put it on his desk, and finish dusting. I'll tell him where it is."

She had no doubt that the girl was honest. Honesty was something she could smell, she always said, like musk. Even Gertrude had been honest enough, though untrustworthy in other ways. This girl was going to be a good worker, she could tell that already. It was a relief, after Gertrude, to have someone to train who only had to be shown once how to do something. But still, Mrs. Barr was sorry it hadn't been Elizabeth. What bliss it would have been to have had one of her own folk there. It had been too much to expect, of course. That was one of the hardships of going into service. You couldn't expect to see much of your family.

Mrs. Barr had prayed for her favourite niece before she slept. It looked like being a hot summer. Elizabeth, with her good looks, that fine complexion, would be less likely to get smallpox if she got a good place. Smallpox and typhoid always seemed to start among the villagers.

It was lucky for Elizabeth, as well as for Doctor Arkwright, the general practitioner in Malton, that he had married the daughter of of a gentleman farmer — albeit against her father's wishes — otherwise the doctor and his wife could not have inhabited such a good house as Millington Lodge, or employed a housekeeper as well as a cook, a lady's maid, two kitchenmaids, two housemaids, a groom and a gardener. It was, after all, "Before Lloyd George put the doctors on their feet", as my grandmother (who was Martha Cousins) used to say.

As one of the housemaids, Charity Lawson, was elderly and ailing, she was sent to her sisters, and the next news was that Elizabeth was to train as a housemaid at Dr. Arkwright's. Mrs. Barr was delighted. It meant that she would see Elizabeth every Sunday evening at the Old Priory Church. Any grudge she had against Martha vanished when she heard the news.

Martha did not see very much of her employers, but she felt happier when Mrs. Marney came into the nursery one evening and told her how pleased Nanny was with her. Nanny had had one of her "turns". She was in bed before the children that night. Martha had taken charge, kept them quiet, bathed them, and tidied up the nursery. They were sitting round the fire having cocoa and ginger biscuits when Mrs. Marney came in to enquire about Nanny.

"Will you sit up with her tonight, Martha?" If she goes to sleep and her breathing is quite regular, you can go to bed. If she has an attack of asthma and can't get her breath, you must wake Mrs. Barr and ask her to send John

41

for Dr. Arkwright."

Responsibilities were heaped on the young Martha which no-one would have dreamed of imposing on such a maid as Gertrude. Nor would the pretty, self-possessed Elizabeth have been quite so thoroughly trusted by a new employer. There was something about Martha that you knew could be depended upon, and moreover, as Mrs. Marney told her husband, she was much above the average intelligence of her class.

Working girls like Martha, of a type that a generation or so later would be studying for university entrance, were in those days described by complacent employers as "quick" - servants who did not have to be shown twice how to do anything.

When she had to sit up with a sick child or with Nanny, Martha was exceedingly grateful when Mr. Marney told her that she could choose a book from the shelves in his study, provided that she took good care of it. When she returned "Oliver Twist", he was amazed that she had read it so quickly, but she answered his questions about the book so well that he was delighted with her, and gave her a florin.

"Martha thrives on responsibility. She is well named," Mr. Marney said at breakfast one morning when Mrs. Marney, who had been to ask how Nanny was, added that Martha looked a bit paler than usual herself. "She isn't getting enough sleep. After all, she is only thirteen!"

Mrs. Marney felt contrite. She thought of Emma, still in bed because she had been allowed to sit up late to finish some embroidery.

Matthew Marney was a large, vigorous, ruddy-faced man who perhaps took his family responsibilities more lightly than his business. He was a good employer, and quick to reward good service.

In appearance he was more like a country

squire than a typical Quaker. His children always went to their father first to ask a favour or to tell him of some trouble, and he always listened. It was Mama who was strict.

Mr. Marney was liberal in every sense of the word, but beneath his open-handedness, his generosity, and his love of humanity, he was a man to whom the faith of his fathers was the corner-stone of his life.

CHAPTER FOUR: MR. GAVIN.

Martha went into the study that morning even more swiftly than usual. She was five minutes late, and minutes were more precious than gold in the morning. That was why her dark hair was not pinned into a bun but left in a pony tail, like the portrait of the young Queen Victoria on an old copper coin.

She went straight across the room to the bay window and opened it. For a second, before she drew up the blind on the south side, she stooped to smell the geranium that stood on the window sill. Her profile, with the well-shaped, smooth dark head, he nose wrinkled as she inhaled, was silhouetted against the pale Holland blind for that brief moment. Most people didn't like the smell of geraniums, but Martha did. She loved their vivid colour, and she loved that strange, peppery scent that seemed to come from somewhere far from the north of Yorkshire.

"You must be Martha Cousins." The voice was gentle, musing, and masculine.

Martha nearly jumped out of her skin. Turning round, she realized that there had been someone sitting in that great leather armchair by the fireside when she had entered the room. It was a gentleman's voice, anyway. It was no intruder. There was no doubt in her mind to whom it belonged. She had heard them saying in the kitchen that the Marney's eldest son was coming home from London.

"Goodness, Mr. Gavin, you gave me such a shock."

He was on his feet now, a slightly built, pale, fair young man with spectacles, smiling at her and shaking hands with that firm grip which resembled his father's. Mercifully, she had not yet blackleaded the kitchen stove. While her

44

own hands were warm and glowing with the bustle of activity since she had risen half an hour earlier, Gavin's were cold.

"I know you're Martha Cousins because I've heard all about you. I hope you're going to be happy with us, Martha, and stay for a long time."

"I hope so, sir. Thank ye very much. I do like it here. Can I get you some breakfast, sir? Or would you rather I got the fire going first?"

"I'll have some tea, if I may. Can I go in the kitchen, Martha? Mrs. Barr isn't up yet, is she?"

"No, sir, and you'll be warmer there. The fire's going nicely. I'll get some tea ready, and I can cook ye some breakfast if you like."

"No, no, Martha. All I want is a cup of tea. Then I'll go upstairs and have a bath. I must have fallen asleep down here. My mother said I would."

Mr. Gavin was unexpected in more ways than one. He was not in the least like any of the others, thought Martha. She hoped he was well, but he was too thin and pale. And while everyone in the family - except Master Reginald - always treated their servants with courtesy, Mr. Gavin, it seemed to Martha, had spoken to her as she thought no employer could speak to a servant - as if he really did care whether she was happy there.

His voice had almost a woman's quality of tenderness in it. He had regular features; he was handsome even, but there was something unworldly, ascetic about him. He looked sensitive and scholarly; he wore spectacles, and did not have side whiskers but was clean-shaven. Nothing could be less like the dashing, dark-haired, whiskered young man whom young girls dreamed of on Midsummer Night, or hoped to dream of.

But it seemed to Martha that she loved Gavin from the first moment she heard his voice. That voice which was full of amusement but also full of kindness. Whatever else he was, she thought, Mr. Gavin was a gentleman.

At this time, his eldest son was causing Mr. Marney the deepest distress. The drudgery of the publisher's office and the intrigues of literary society had disillusioned the over-sensitive Gavin, who would probably have been happier at Oxford – but Quakers did not go to Oxford. He had come home because he was ill with nervous exhaustion and because he had to tell his parents he could no longer subscribe to their faith.

In London, he had gone to church with a friend who knew that, although a Quaker, Gavin was interested in the architecture of old churches and cathedrals. The ceremonies and rituals which the Quakers despised had come to mean a kind of liberation for Gavin. It was the "absolute freedom" of the Quaker faith which now seemed to him rigid and formal. He had come home to tell his parents of his irrevocable decision to become a member of the Church of England.

For Mr. Marney, a man who as a father was unusually easy-going and tolerant, this was a crisis of a kind he had never dreamed of. He would have been prepared to pay his son's debts if he had got into debt; he would have listened sympathetically if a woman had been involved. He had even hoped that after all his son was coming home to ask if he could stay there and go into the bank.

When Gavin's quiet, courteous voice had made it perfectly clear to his father that it was useless to argue further, the banker, after a long silence, could only repeat with profound bitterness: "The third generation ... The third generation."

He had gone to bed at last leaving Gavin alone in the study, aware of a loneliness that would be far worse while he was with his family than when he was in London. He had sat by the dying fire for almost an hour without moving. He felt very weary, very much alone, but unafraid. He knew his voyage of self-discovery had begun.

He thought about Josephine Saunders. He knew now that, after all, he had not given her up because he lacked the strength of mind to oppose his family. It was because he hadn't been so much in love with her that nothing else mattered.

He had gone to London, and six months later Josephine, whose family worshipped at St. Mary's church, had married Richard Easterby, the eldest son of a gentleman farmer.

ST. MARY'S PRIORY CHURCH
OLD MALTON.

MARILYN WHITE

CHAPTER FIVE: THE PRIORY.

On her first Sunday at The Mount, Mrs. Barr had said briskly to Martha half an hour before it was time to set off for church: "Your aunt would wish you to go to a place of worship on the Sabbath, Martha. Get ready and you can come with us."

Martha knew it was not possible for her to go to the meeting at Norton, it was too far away, but she wasn't at all sure that her relatives would approve of her going to the Priory.

Martha had never been in St. Mary's Priory Church in Malton before. Compared with the homely intimacy and the warm welcome of the Methodists, who met in the house of a small farmer, it was quite a terrifying experience, going to church.

They waited until the gentry had been excorted down the aisle by the verger, the doors of their pews unlocked, the women servants whispering together about the Squire's Lady's new pelisse or milady's new bonnet. Everything in the Priory was rich and splendid and awe-inspiring to Martha, especially the people.

The Quakers, however rich, dressed plainly, although their clothes were well cut. These fine ladies swept down the aisle in crinolines of glowing dark red or lilac silk, trimmed with lace, exquisite bonnets tied with satin ribbons, and marvellous, fringed Indian shawls or pelisses trimmed with ostrich feathers or fur.

Evening service was nothing to the spectacle of the morning church parade, but it was a dazzling array of fashion to Martha's eyes. Sitting at last with the other servants at the back of the old church, she could not but see what a comtrast they were in their dark grey or black calico, with one or two of the older women like Mrs. Barr wearing black silk.

There were other servants there like herself for whom attendance at evening service was compulsory. One or two elderly women nodded off during the sermon. Martha sighed as she remembered what the women had to face tomorrow. Monday, wash-day, was the hardest day of a servant's week.

When she knelt to pray she prayed with all her heart and soul for her own folk and longed to be with them. She could not find her place in the Book of Common Prayer, and Mrs. Barr and Elizabeth did not help her, and she did not know any of the hymns.

But the Priory was beautiful, with the evening sunshine streaming through the stained glass windows. And when the vicar read from the Bible, she heard words then which she had heard before, and then the vision of the simple white-washed room at the farm, the kind faces, the fervent singing of her aunt's favourite hymn "The Old Rugged Cross", rose before her and she was more homesick than ever.

She hated going to church with Mrs. Barr and Elizabeth, who was condescending, and she thought how Aunt Lizzie would have disapproved of the showy ribbons on Elizabeth's bonnet. She even wore her hair, one Sunday, with curls on her forehead like the Princess of Wales. Mrs. Barr did not approve of this: it was a style of hairdressing not to be copied by a servant.

Martha, not possessing a bonnet, was compelled to wear a black shawl over her dark grey calico. The bodice of the dress was trimmed with a simple design of jet beads embroidered by Nanny. She had insisted on doing this one evening in the nursery. It was Nanny's way of showing gratitude for all that Martha did for her. She could not have refused such a gift. The beads sparkled in the light of the

50

great brass oil lamps hanging from the roof of the Priory Church.

Martha's looks had improved a great deal since she went to live at The Mount. Good food, more fresh air, and better living conditions had helped her grow into a girl who was comely if not pretty. Her skin had a glow, even if it would never be pink and white like Elizabeth's. Her hair shone with life like her eyes. When she was looking her best there was something striking about her appearance which Mrs. Barr called "foreign", but Martha did not mind her saying that.

She knew she had a great grandmother who was half French. She had heard tales about her, about the farm somewhere near Scarborough, and about the very old lady who wore fine lace. Martha was proud of her French blood.

It was not long before Martha was made aware that, although Elizabeth considered her a fright and she had heard Mrs. Barr say: "She's a funny-looking girl", not everyone thought she was ugly.

The coachmen, grooms, and stable-boys sat behind the gentry to whose establishment they belonged. Then, at the back of the church, servants from smaller households such as Mrs. Barr and Elizabeth and Martha sat in pews which were not rented.

Most of the young women servants were well-made and had fine complexions. A few of them even sat in church with their sweethearts, young men who were also in service, although not of course in the same household - that would never be permitted.

There were farm labourers, the shepherd from Manor Farm, and two young men who had the most glamorous jobs of all and could take their pick of the girls - if only there had been time and opportunity for courting. Stanley James and

Roderick Dark were railwaymen on the new Malton-Driffield line.

Being a railwayman was a novel, romantic occupation, much better than being a footman or a groom. Many more men applied than could be taken on, and every railwayman, from the humblest porter to the driver of "Gladstone" or "Antelope" was proud of his job and completely dedicated to serving the public.

The best tribute to the railwaymen of that age is in the letter Charlotte Bronte wrote to her publisher, S.W. Williams, from No. 2 Cliff, Scarborough, on May 27, 1849.

"I am thankful to say," wrote Charlotte, "we reached our destination safely, having rested one night at York.... We found assistance wherever we needed it: there was always an arm ready to do for my sister what I was not strong enough to do: lift her in and out of the carriage, carry her across the line, etc. It made her happy to see both York and its Minster, and Scarborough and the bay once more."

Her sister Anne, dying of consumption, frail and emaciated, had achieved her last wish of seeing Scarborough again before she died there - on May 29 - thanks to the railwaymen who looked after her on that last journey from Haworth.

The young women servants, however demurely their eyes were cast down as they filed out of the church after the gentry, were very well aware of the eager, supplicating eyes of the young men.

Chances of making acquaintance with the opposite sex were so hedged round by their employers' rules and taboos that going to church was one of the few opportunities a young woman in service had of being seen by young men outside her place of work, where it was impossible to escape the eye of her superiors.

Sometimes a determined lover, if he was literate, would manage miraculously to slip a note inside a hymnbook: "I think you are very pretty. Can I walk a little way with you after church. I will wait by the fir trees."

The note, of course, was in Elizabeth's hymnbook. It was signed "R. Dark".

The fir trees were at the corner of Moor Lane, where Elizabeth usually said goodbye to her aunt. Elizabeth was a year older than Martha. She looked at least sixteen. No-one was surprised when they saw her walking back to the Arkwright's house with a young man - and some of the other women servants envied her. Roderick Dark was a tall, broad-shouldered young man of twenty with a frank, open face and a fine black beard and whiskers.

"She'll 'ave ti start saving hup, now she's got a sweetheart. She wain't 'ave money for a new bonnet this year," the cook at The Mount commented. Sweethearts like Elizabeth and Roderick did not get much time together when the girl was in service. They had to look forward to the dark nights of winter when they could stand under the trees near Millington Lodge and kiss without other people's eyes on them. But these kisses could not last long, because Elizabeth was expected back from evening service in time to take supper into the master and mistress.

So they looked further ahead and planned to get married - when they had saved up enough. With her sovereign a year at Martinmas and his twelve sovereigns, it would still be a long time before they could set up home together - especially as Elizabeth found it so hard to resist buying something pretty for herself whenever she had any money.

Martha found Elizabeth a little less unfriendly, now that she was in love. She even

53

repeated to Martha one day that she had heard one of the grooms at the Squire's say to Roderick: "What do they call the little black-haired beauty that lives at the Quakers?"

Martha was not as pleased as Elizabeth had expected she would be to hear that she had an admirer. She did not care much for the stares, admiring or otherwise, of the grooms and footmen who sat through the service behind their employers, looking bored and cynical.

The particular stable lad who had asked for her name was a good-looking, dark-haired lad of Irish extraction. He was a lapsed Catholic who preferred going to the Priory with the rest of his household to going on his own to Mass. His eyes appraised the women and girls at the back of the church as expertly as his master, the Squire, judged horseflesh.

It was true that young Martha's first dreams of love had always held visions of a lover who was dark-haired and dark-eyed. Perhaps this was due to childish affection: her father had had dark hair, and, in fact, none of her family were blonde. She had always said to herself that when she married her husband must be dark.

Martha had learned to read when she was six years old. At that age she read fairy tales, and she had come to believe absolutely that one day a fairy prince would come to marry her. Unfortunately, she announced this as a fact one morning to her family.

"Martha's going to marry a prince!" became her brothers' favourite way of teasing poor Martha.

As brothers so often do, they had not been able to resist playing a trick on their little sister which was really unkind. One Sunday evening, Martha was allowed to go to a meeting at the farmhouse where the Methodists met, although she was only a little girl of seven. A missionary from the Hull Circuit was coming to speak about his experience on the Gold Coast.

Standing as near as he could get to the bright flames of the fire, six feet tall and as black as coal, an Ashanti brave was introduced to the villagers by the missionary. "My friend, dear brothers and sisters, is a prince in his own country," repeated the Rev. MacDonald.

Whatever the missionary went on to tell them about the Gold Coast Martha never knew. Her brother Walter nudged her and whispered in her ear, very seriously: "See, Martha. you were right. Your prince has come for you!" Martha disgraced herself by bursting into tears, and had to be taken home.

Until she met Gavin Marney, Martha had thought she could never fall in love with anyone with fair hair and blue eyes, but in spite of herself she had! He was her first real love.

Perhaps if it had not been for Gavin, she would have gone on being attracted to dark-haired men all her life, in which case she would never have married my grandfather, Ben Smith, whose colouring was as Anglo-Saxon as hers was Latin.

It had not occurred to Gavin Marney to wonder what Martha's family might think about her attending service at the Priory, or to consider what she might be feeling herself — until that evening when he came into the church a few seconds late. He found himself looking for Martha, and he was struck by the mute unhappiness on her face as she gazed at the altar. He remembered then that the Cousins family were Methodists.

Gavin usually went to St. Mary's in the gig. One evening on the way back to The Mount he overtook Martha, who was walking alone, her shawl clasped tightly round her against the icey

east wind. "Poor little peasant," he thought,
seeing the sturdy figure resolutely plodding on
towards the home where she still had so many
duties to perform.

She reminded him of women he had seen in
Italy. She had their simple dignity, he
thought, but her face as he remembered it in the
church had not that look of rapt devotion, of
spiritual serenity, he had seen on the faces in
the cathedral. No wonder, if she had been
separated from her own people and their way of
worship. He did not like to think that his
mother's servants were herded together for
compulsary attendance at the Priory by the
housekeeper, regardless of their convictions.

So that was the first question he asked her
as soon as she had climbed into the gig and he
had flicked the whip to set the pony trotting
briskly again. "Martha, I thought your family
were Primitive Methodists. Don't you ever go to
the meetings now?"

Martha's cheeks had more colour in them
than usual. They were glowing with the cold air
and also with the happiness that always filled
her being when she was with Mr. Gavin. She did
not feel shy: she always felt at ease with
every member of the Marney family now. In her
secret heart she knew that, although in the
kitchen she was at the bottom of the domestic
hierarchy, to her employers she was a valued
servant.

She loved her new home and the people in
it. She got as much satisfaction as her
mistress from seeing a room that was well-kept,
warm, and welcoming, with everything in its
place, a bright fire burning and plenty of coal
and logs in their rosy copper containers. Why
shouldn't she strive with all her strength to
help Mrs. Marney run her home?

"Yes, sir, my people are Methodys, but the

meetings are at Norton, you see."

"But don't you miss going to the meetings very much, Martha. Or are you perfectly happy about attending service at the Priory?"

She could not lie to him. She bit her lip, but she had to answer somehow. She raised her eyes to Gavin's: "No, Mr. Gavin, not entirely. It is strange to me, sir."

He could not stop himself from saying, a little grimly: "And to me, Martha, but I have chosen to worship there, and it seems you have not. You should not be compelled to attend evening service at the Priory, unless you wish to be confirmed in the Church of England as I do. It is only right that you should be allowed to attend the meeting with your own people. Would you like me to take you in the gig to Norton next Sunday?"

Martha's eyes were bright with tears. Such an offer just after she had experienced that terrible feeling of isolation and loneliness at the Priory was almost too great a joy to bear.

Looking at her with his intent gaze, Gavin understood her silence with the quick sympathy that was one of the things she loved in him. He put his hand on hers for a moment: "Come, Martha, we'll see my mother about it as soon as we get home."

Gavin's words had made her supremely happy. The thought of seeing her own folk next Sunday – Mrs. Marney had agreed to Martha going once a month to the meeting, if the gig could be spared – made her feel like singing as she went about the house, only, of course, well-trained servants in a Quaker household did not do such things.

Remembering all that Gavin had said to her, she realised that she knew the answer to something that had puzzled them a good deal in the kitchen. The servants had decided, in

57

common with some of the neighbours of the Marneys, that Mr. Gavin's mysterious illness and his attendance at the Priory could only have been brought about by one thing: he had never got over his affair with Josephine. So often do gossips put the cart before the horse.

"Mr. Gavin would never have gone off to London, if it hadn't been for her," Martha heard Cook say. "That minx unsettled him. She wain't good enough for him, anyway, and she's married on the rebound. Mr. Richard may be as rich as Mr. Gavin, but he wain't make her a good husband. He's allus been a wild one."

Martha believed what Gavin had told her. He had gone to the Priory because he wished to worship God in his own way. She had seen Josephine and Gavin greet each other, and Martha did not think they looked as if they were still in love. She admired Josephine, a dark-haired beauty, but she thought she looked cross and spoilt. She was glad she had not married Mr. Gavin.

Well, if Mr. Gavin had chosen the Church of England, there must be something to be said for it, she supposed, thinking once more of what he had told her when they were in the gig. It was not the kind of worship that appealed to her, but everybody must decide for themselves, as he had said.

Martha did not enter the Priory Church at Old Malton again until December 16th, 1872, when she was married there to her handsome, fair-haired lover, who was, of course, Ben Smith.

CHAPTER SIX: THE MEETING AT NORTON.

When he took her to the meeting at Norton, it was Gavin's last Sunday at home. Early the next morning he would take the train for London.

So Martha's joy in meeting her family, her pleasure in the company of Mr. Gavin as they drove there in the gig had a bitter-sweet edge. She was deliciously and acutely aware of each moment, and of its passing.

Martha had managed to get a message delivered to her home by the carrier. It was lucky for her that he had called that week, and that she had been in the kitchen when he did.

All her family were there - her aunt and uncle, Mark and Walter, who used to tease her so much, were with their sweethearts, Charity Beckett and Mary Rabbit, and her cousin Tilly already looked more grown-up. She was the eldest girl at home now, even if she was only twelve. All the "bairns" were there too.

Martha's eyes were as bright with tears now as they had been when she left home, but today they could fall unheeded as she embraced them all.

There had been no tears in her eyes when Mr. Gavin helped her down from the gig outside the farmhouse. Eager as she was to see her family, she had been aware for those seconds only of him, and of the curious eyes of the Ranters seeing her, Martha Cousins, drive up in a gig, driven by a gentleman, the Marneys' eldest son. She heard him say kindly: "The gig will come for you at eight o'clock. God bless you, Martha," then she heard the clip-clop of the hooves going away over the cobbles.

It was a sound she could hardly bear to hear, reminding her of tomorrow when he would be going away. She thought she could never love anyone as she loved Mr. Gavin. For a second she was half afraid of meeting her family, of letting them see the heartbreak in her eyes.

Then she was in Aunt Lizzie's arms. Her aunt was answering the stunned look of disbelief she had seen in Martha's first look. "I lost the bairn, love. I'm a'reet now. It was God's will."

To a woman with so many children, an occasional miscarriage was not a tragedy, but Martha looked anxiously at her aunt's altered figure. Aunt Lizzie looked pale and drawn, with shadows under her eyes. "She's looking so much older!" Martha thought.

Her aunt's back had been slightly bent for as long as she remembered, with nursing children, carrying them, rocking them in the cradle that was always next to her bed. Martha's eyes filled with tears of love and pity. "Is Tilly doing for ye alreet, Aunt?"

"Ay, lass, our Tilly's looking hafter us. Dain't ye want ti gi' yer uncle a kiss, then?"

Her uncle looked as hearty and strong and weatherbeaten as always. He kissed her, and then held her at arm's length, looking at his niece with a pride and fondness that made her suddenly shy, with their Ranter friends all about them.

"Tha's making a grand lass, our Martha. Ah knew tha would. Tha's getting plenty o' grub at Quakers, ony road."

"Come, Robert, we mun get sat down." There were so many of the Cousins family that it took two benches to seat them all.

Martha was thankful to see the "bairns" all looking well, and how very clean and smart they were. Somebody had been busy washing and scrubbing, and darning and patching.

"Ah diz all ye did, n' more, our Martha," Tilly whispered. "Ah was hup at five today, wain't Ah, Mam, going for t' water to wash bairns. Dain't they look bonny, now?"

Of course, the difference in the "bairns" was as remarkable as the growth of healthy young children always is when you have not seen them for months. Tilly had certainly made as sure as she could that they were all "fit" - a Yorkshire word usually applied to crops, but sometimes to such a fine and numerous family as the young Cousins.

Their cheeks shone with carbolic, their hair had been washed, and they all wore clean clothes and well-shone boots. Tilly had sat up darning stockings and mending rents. Her young brothers had been slapped and scalded and somehow induced to stay clean and tidy for the reunion with Martha. Young James, who seemed to have a natural attraction for dirt, looked at Martha with big reproachful dark eyes. He had mixed feelings about meeting his cousin if it meant so much soap and water beforehand.

"Eh, whativver's to do wi' ye, Jamie? Yer looking that solemn. Wain't ye give me a kiss?" Martha slipped back into the old North Riding speech with her cousins.

It was pure bliss, being with her own folk again, and she thanked God that their meeting had not been allowed by her mistress only because there was a funeral in the family. That was the sole reason most employers would consider allowing a servant to see relations, except at Martinmas. Yes, she was lucky. She was happy that Sunday evening early in December 1862, at the Methodist meeting in Norton.

She sang the well-known hymns by Wesley with a heart full of thanksgiving, and she joined in the chorus of "Hallelujah!" and "Praise the Lord!" with more enthusiasm than she had ever done before. It was a miracle, being there with her own people.

But there were some things that struck her

forcibly since she had attended the last meeting. Looking at the women, she did not expect to see fashionable bonnets or fur-trimmed pelisses, but it seemed to her that the servants who sat at the back of the Priory on Sunday evenings did not look quite so drab as some of the women here, and, of course, even servants could keep themselves clean with all that hot water. The smell of humanity here was overwhelming.

She would be sorry if there were no time to talk with her family, to tell Aunt Lizzie the story of those jet beads, which she could see from the look in her eye troubled her.

Oddly enough, the extremely strict rules about dress which were followed so rigidly by the Primitive Methodists at this time had been promulgated by one of the founders of the sect, William Clowes, who, before his conversion, had been in his way something of a dandy.

A descendant of Josiah Wedgewood, Clowes had been a skilled potter who earned as much as £1 a week in 1803. "I wore a coat and pantaloons of the best superfine, with yellow buttons, ordered from a tailor in Hull," he recorded in his journal. After a drunken brawl at the "Dog and Duck" he narrowly escaped being a victim of the Press Gang by the intervention of his master. The next day he set off for Tunstall.

"I prayed if he would carry me safely to my native place, I would then serve Him.... No sooner had I arrived at journey's end than among my old companions my promises were forgotten.... Sometimes I used to walk in solitary and unfrequented places, wishing I were a bird or a beast or anything else not accountable to the tribune of heaven.... I started out of sleep, afraid of seeing the room full of devils and damned spirits ... and wished for day, to drown my distressing convictions with drink."

A friend took him to a love-feast, and the next day he went to a prayer meeting. "While all was excitement and noise around I wrestled as one alone with my Maker till I felt the bonds which held me breaking.... What is this? I asked myself. This is what Methodists mean by being converted.... In an agony of prayer I believed God would save me - then I believed He was saving me - then I believed He had saved me, and it was so."

Martha was glancing anxiously at the grandfather clock in the corner near the staircase when she recognised the firm, clear tones of Martin Summers.

Martin was a class leader of the Methodists and a local preacher. He usually offered the closing prayers. They were always short, simple, and dignified, thanking God for His mercies and asking for His guidance in the days to come. "He's a good man, Martin is, but he nivver gets carried away wi' t' spirit," some of them used to say, pityingly. Others said he was too much under the thumb of his wife.

Whatever happened, she must not keep the gig waiting. They were singing the closing hymn "When I survey the wondrous cross" when Martha rose, pressed Aunt Lizzie's hand, smiled at her uncle and the children and slipped out into the cold, fresh air.

"Ay, Ah thought Ranters'd still be at it," said Giles Lazenby, who was driving the gig. Gavin had gone straight home from the service at St. Mary's, to spend as much time as he could with his family on his last night at Malton.

Martha said nothing, but she shivered a little as she sat beside Giles in the gig and pulled her shawl closely around her. She was still in spirit beside her own folk in the meeting as they drove through the narrow streets, then the Market Square in Malton and more narrow streets until finally they reached the broad road that led to The Mount.

It was one of her last duties on a Sunday night to put cold tea from the pot in the kitchen on some of the plants that stood on the wide window sill. Cold tea was good for geraniums, and nothing is ever wasted in a Quaker household.

There was no-one in the study when she went in. She always looked at the huge leather chair now to make sure, and she was thinking regretfully that she would not see Mr. Gavin again, when he entered the room.

It is possible that seeing her there by the plants she was tending, Gavin remembered how he had first seen Martha in that room. After asking her how she had found her family, he added: "Do you know, Martha, that when I was in London someone told me that the geranium is Charles Dickens' favourite flower. What do you think of that, eh?"

Gavin had been to hear him read a scene from one of his bestsellers - the death of Nancy from "Oliver Twist". It had been too melodramatic for his taste, but, during the reading or rather the acting of the drama, he had been incapable of criticism, of suspending belief.

"If Charles Dickens hadn't been a writer, I am sure he would have been equally successful on the stage," Gavin added. "Do you know, Martha, that at Christmas the Dickens family spend most of their time producing elaborate amateur theatricals? He even has friends in the acting profession who go and assist."

Mr. Marney had come in and heard some of this conversation. He was not pleased to hear his son talking to a girl of Martha's age about the theatre. Mr. Marney had aged in the last

64

few months. He stood, frowning, his brow deeply furrowed. If only Gavin had never gone to London! His thoughts were as clearly communicated to his son as if they had been spoken.

To Martha, the room seemed colder since he had come in, in spite of its bright fire, rich velvet curtains and the warm glow of the oil lamps. She spoke first, trying to break the spell: "Is there anything you require, please, Mr. Marney?"

"No, thank you, Martha, nothing at all. You may go to bed. We shall all be up early in the morning, no doubt." That was his only reference to Gavin's departure.

"Thank you, sir. Goodnight, sir. Goodnight, Mr. Gavin, sir." In a voice she tried not quite successfully to keep steady she added: "Thank you very much for taking me to the meeting, sir."

Gavin gave her a kind smile. "Be a good girl, Martha."

He didn't know, but falling in love with him had made his advice almost unnecessary. Martha was preserved, through her romantic love for Mr. Gavin, from any desire to emulate Elizabeth and take a sweetheart. All she wanted was to devote herself to serving his family - to the end of her days if possible.

Martha's ambition had been shaped during those first months at The Mount. She vowed she would never marry unless she could live the sort of well-ordered life she had known in that household. She didn't think this at all likely, not being a reader of Cook's novelettes, where maids-of-all-work contrived, by most unlikely chances, to end up as duchesses.

CHAPTER SEVEN: MR. HENRY.

"Goodbye, Gavin. God bless you! By God, I wish you were not going back to London!"

His father's emotion, and the oath, were equally surprising to Gavin, as they stood on the platform early next morning waiting for the Hull train. He could hardly believe his ears, but as they gripped hands, he saw the look in his father's eyes and never forgot it. Of course, if he had known then, he would have stayed.

Mr. Marney knew at that moment that his eldest son was the one person in the world to whom he could have trusted his secret, but it was too late: they heard the roar of the train approaching. He stood for a long time after the train had vanished, looking after it as if his eyes could will his son back.

Then he returned home, to face again his private hell of uncertainty, alone.

Martha had known that Mr. Henry was going to be the black sheep of the family long before any of the Marneys had any hint of the trouble he would cause them.

It had happened so many times in that house that Martha had found gold sovereigns, silver florins, and copper coins left on tables or on the mantlepiece. Mr. Marney was very careless, but he had always believed that he could trust everyone in his house implicitly.

One morning when Martha went into the study, she was surprised to see Mr. Henry down even earlier. He had been into the study for a book, he told her quickly. She knew he was lying. He had been taking some of the money from the mantlepiece, for she had seen him put some of it back when he heard her enter.

She was shocked and worried. Everybody liked Mr. Henry: he was so good-looking and good-natured, he had a quick sense of humour that had often made her laugh, and he was Mr. Gavin's brother. It was unthinkable. She wished she had not gone in just then, but she had seen the look on his face as he heard her come in, and the hand going to the mantlepiece and that heap of gold.

Martha knew she would have to tell the housekeeper what she had seen. If money was missing, someone else might be suspected of dishonesty, and that would mean ruin for a servant. She did not let herself think what it might mean for Mr. Henry if he were found out.

Her best opportunity to speak to Mrs. Barr in private would be in the afternoon, when she retired to her room for an hour before tea. Martha was kept particularly busy that morning. One of the maids had been allowed to go home, for the funeral of a young brother. There was diptheria in Malton that winter, and Martha worried about her family and almost dreaded the carrier calling.

Sometime that morning Martha had to go down into the cellars and into one of the huge pantries where meat was kept on marble slabs in a room with a north-facing window. It was always cool and dark in there.

She had her back to the window and was going towards the meat safe when she heard a quick step. Mr. Henry had his arm round her waist, one hand on her breast. He pulled her very close and kissed her hard on the mouth.

Martha responded as passionately, struggling to free herself and giving him a resounding slap on the cheek.

"Don't be a silly girl, Martha. Just give me a kiss, that's all. You're such a little charmer. You have a sweetheart somewhere, haven't you?" His breath had a smell that was not quite unfamiliar to Martha. Even Methodists and Quakers in those days made home-brewed wine.

"If you touch me again, Mr. Henry, I'll scream so they'll hear me in the kitchen. They'll be coming to see what I'm doing as t'is."

"You're a little vixen, Martha, but I like you. You've got something about you, Martha, that'll drive a man mad someday. I didn't mean to hurt you, you know. Say you'll forgive me, won't you? And Martha, do something for me, please."

She knew what was coming.

"Don't tell anyone I was down early today, will ye? If you don't promise I'll not let you go again!"

"I heard cellar door. You'll have to get out while you can, Mr. Henry."

He climbed through one of the windows in that wilderness of cellars and store-places that led into the back garden. She pushed her hair behind her ears and smoothed her dress. At least he had not made her promise.

It made her heart sick to think that one of Gavin's brothers could behave like that. She was sure now that he had taken some of his father's money from the mantlepiece earlier that morning in the study.

Mrs. Barr found it hard to believe that Mr. Henry would be capable of taking the money. He was doing so well at the bank. His father trusted him with so much responsibility, and besides, Mr. Marney would never refuse him if he asked for anything.

"Don't you think, Martha, it might have been some of his own money?" But then why should he put some of it back so hurriedly when he heard her come in? Both women knew it was always Mr. Marney who left money about like that. Whenever a servant took coins found in some odd place to Mrs. Marney, it was always:

68

"Oh, yes, thank you. That will be Mr. Marney's."

Night after night, Mr. Marney stayed late at the bank, long after all his employees, including his son Henry, had gone. He had to be there alone; he had to make perfectly sure whether suspicions he had about certain discrepancies were well-founded or, as he hoped and prayed, due only to carelessness.

The Victorians may have deserved to be called hypocrites on many matters, but at least on this issue, dishonesty, the code was the same for a rich man's son as for his servant. There could be no second chance for a servant who stole from his master, however small the theft, however great the temptation. Discovery inevitably brought dismissal and disgrace.

Mr. Marney knew that, if it were proved that Henry had altered the numbers purposely, with intent to defraud, there was only one course open to him. He must give his son a one-way ticket to Australia, with the minimum amount of money to assist him when he arrived.

Even Mr. Charles Dickens had one "unsatisfactory" son who, when he proved irresponsible about money was sent to the other side of the world.

In those days, when the journey by sea was so long and hazardous, even in the "Warrior", the first sailing ship to be built of iron, when communications were so uncertain, it meant banishment for ever from family and friends and a decent way of life. It was often, in fact, a sentence of death.

Well-educated, charming young men like Henry Marney were frequently never heard of again. They were seldom the type to hold their own with the illiterate, quick-shooting, card-sharping roughnecks who could survive and sometimes even strike it rich in the outback.

Perhaps they were robbed and murdered because they looked as if they would have money on them, or they took to drink, soon became penniless and died of fever or syphilis in some uncaring shanty town.

There came a time when Matthew Marney was compelled to tell his wife that his worst fears about Henry were confirmed. Mrs. Marney's dark hair turned white the night her husband told her. She lay in her room for almost a week, remembering his childhood so vividly that when Henry came to see her for the first time she thought he was a stranger.

His mother remembered how mischievous and lively he had been, how he looked like an angel when he was asleep, such a beautiful child, with fair hair and those long, dark lashes. She remembered how he always took longer to get up than the others, how once when he was called he had said: "I'll come when I've finished this dream."

It was a good thing Martin and Reginald were both away at school in York. Emma was the only one of the children who knew the truth, and although she did not resemble her eldest brother Gavin in looks, being dark like her mother, she had some of his quiet strength of character. Emma helped her mother to be calm and to go on trusting in God, somehow. But Martha was the one she sent for when she did not want any of the family to see her.

Martha often found Mrs. Marney sobbing now when she answered her bell, and the poor woman confided more of her inmost thoughts and fears to the very young Martha than she did to her nearest friends and relations.

It was a heavy burden for a young girl to bear, especially one as sensitive and as devoted to the family as Martha was. She thought it was terrible that there could be no reprieve for

this handsome, feckless son of the Marneys, but
she knew such things had to be. She prayed that
if she had sons one day not one of them would be
dishonest.

They could not let poor Nanny know why he
was going. Her health was too precarious.
Henry told her he was tired of the bank and he
was going to Australia to be a sheep-farmer.
She exclaimed in amazement, but she never
doubted his word.

"You'll have to get up early every morning,
Master Henry, if you're going to be a farmer.
But I expect you'll do very well, only I wish it
wain't so far away. I only hopes I lives to see
ye come back, rich."

"So do I, Nanny." He was more affectionate
and docile with Nanny now than he had ever been.
He spent a lot of time sitting with her in the
nursery before he went away, but he was
irritable with young Sarah and Edgar when they
asked him questions about sheep-farming.

There were no passports to apply for. No
red tape held up travellers in those days: they
only had to obtain information about when the
next ship would leave Southampton for
Freemantle. Mr. Marney would go to Hull to see
Henry off on the London train, then he would
return alone and go to his office at the bank,
meet his staff, talk to customers, and go home
earlier than he had been doing because the
bank's affairs were in order now.

Henry would be met by Gavin in London.
They would travel to Southampton together, and
then Henry would face that voyage, and
Australia, alone.

Martha knelt to say her prayers every night
now in her room under the eaves. She prayed for
her own family, but especially for the Marneys
in their trouble, and for Henry. She was still
on her knees when there was a tap on the door.

"Oh, God, Mr. Henry." She spoke the words in a whisper.

"Let me in, Martha, for God's sake, or I'll shoot myself." He looked lost and lonely and frightened, more like a little boy looking for Nanny than a young man who must have a girl in his arms.

She let him in and closed the door. For a minute they clung to each other and she felt his tears on her cheeks. He didn't attempt to kiss her at first, and just for a few moments Martha, poor innocent, believed that all he desired that night was her company.

"I couldn't stand being alone tonight, Martha." She remembered those words afterwards with bitterness. He hadn't even pretended that he loved her.

A few minutes later and Martha had sunk onto her bed, tired and overwrought with all she had been through. Mr. Henry was kneeling, but he wasn't praying. He was caressing her feet, which were very cold. It did not surprise Henry to find that Martha had such pretty feet, narrow, with a high arched instep, and graceful ankles. He had always thought she had a fine figure, and he had noted her well-shaped arms once when he had gone into the scullery and seen her with her sleeves rolled above the elbow one wash-day. "You've got a dancer's foot, Martha. Pity you're a Methodist."

What marvellous legs she had, but he could always tell what the legs would be like from the figure and the shape of the arms. Henry had already boasted of his conquest of Martha to his gaming companions in Hull. "My mother has a little maid who has French blood. She's passionate all right." He hadn't thought it would take him so long to seduce Martha.

He had her in his arms now. He was kissing her and pleading with her between his kisses.

72

"Martha, please, please, don't send me away.
You can't think what it is to feel everyone in
the world has turned against you. Try to be
kind to me, Martha. I'm so unhappy."

There was no comfort in that cold little
room except in Martha's bed. His fingers were
undoing the buttons of her high-necked cotton
nightdress. "Take it off, Martha."

They were naked now in her bed, but they
were not cold. Their two healthy young bodies
were warming each other. She pitied him so
much, and she did love him more than a little,
because she loved all his family. But she knew
that what she was doing was wrong, and she was
not made happy by their love-making as he was.

There was more of pain than of pleasure in
Martha's deflowering, but it was not rape.
Henry was and always would be attractive to
women, but for a time she writhed and moaned in
his arms, and he heard her murmur his brother's
name, "Gavin", but he didn't question her.

"You're a lovely girl, Martha. I'll never
forget you." That at least was one promise Henry
kept.

He was asleep before she was, for there
were things that Martha had to do. She had bled
a great deal, and she must put the sheet to soak
in cold water. "Thank God cold water brings
blood out so quick!" he heard her murmur just
before he slept.

Only a few years later, when he lay dying
from a gunshot wound, Henry would hear a woman's
voice saying the same words as she plunged his
shirt into a bowl. The girl, Rose Hartford,
from the saloon at Kerang, wondered who "Martha"
was. She was a kind girl, and she wished she
could have written to her, as he had died with
that name on his lips, but Rose could not read
or write.

"What the hell? What an infernal noise!

73

Can't you stop it, Martha?" The clash of the great iron bell that summoned Martha so early was an unknown sound to Mr. Henry's ears, and a very unwelcome one, the next morning.

She made him get up and go down to his room before she went into the kitchen, but when she went down, a few seconds later, he was sitting huddled by the kitchen fire, his head in his hands, paler than she was.

The fire had been well banked up the night before, and everything had been made ready for his early departure. Martha poked the fire into a blaze and put the kettle on.

Later that morning, when he left home, Henry gave his mother the brilliant smile that made him the handsomest of all her children, then he kissed her and told her to bear up, because he would write to her, often. But in the kitchen, having tea with Martha, he let the tears stream down his face.

Whatever torment Henry endured on his first week on board the "Alexandra", it cannot have been compared with what Martha lived through that week.

She slept very little for six nights after Mr. Henry went away. Her mind was racked by terrible fears of the future as soon as she lay down in that bed. Supposing she was pregnant? Mrs. Marney would send her home with a letter to her aunt. Nobody would believe how it had happened. They would think that she and Mr. Henry had been carrying on. They would say she was no better than Gertrude. She would have to leave the baby with Aunt Lizzie and go to the hiring fair to get another place.

Thinking of Gertrude reminded her of Gavin. She knew some stupid people still thought that Gavin had seduced Gertrude, and they might think he was the father of Martha's baby, because he had driven her to Norton in the gig. Gavin, who would no more have taken advantage of a servant in his mother's house than he would have taken his father's money. How he would despise her for what she had done.

Her mental agony was extreme. She understood now in those dark hours how a girl like Hetty Sorrell in "Adam Bede" could drown her baby - alone, friendless, ill, forced to beg in the streets.

On the seventh night she slept so soundly that she did not hear the great iron bell crashing over her head in the morning. Mrs. Barr came to see what had happened, alarmed because she thought Martha must be ill. But she was only a little faint, and very thankful. She hadn't known until then whether what had happened to Gertrude had happened to her, Martha Cousins.

CHAPTER EIGHT: STEPHEN.

Martha had to face alone the shadow that Henry had cast over her life. Her innocence, her complete lack of experience had played its part in her betrayal, but she did not blame Henry so much as she blamed herself for having been insane enough to let him into her room that night.

How could she let any young man court her thinking she was something that she was not? No decent man would marry her now. She would be content if she could stay and serve the Marney family all her days. God had been more merciful to her than he had been to poor Gertrude.

But, wherever she went now, Martha was finding that young men went out of their way to talk to her, however little encouragement she gave them.

When she met her Aunt Lizzie for the first time after Mr. Henry went away, she had clung to her as if she couldn't bear to let her go. Her passionate love for the family and her animation when she was with them, in contrast to her shy reserve with other members of the congregation, were observed by the student preacher that Sunday at the meeting. He noticed also, when she was introduced to him by Lilah, that Martha spoke a more refined language than the family he supposed then she had been born into.

Stephen Elvidge Blakeston was one of the first probationary Methodist ministers to have a tutor assigned by the Manchester district where he lived. The Rev. John McPherson met students fortnightly to examine them in the scriptures. One day, through this man's ambition, there would be a Methodist college at Manchester, although the first one would be Elmfield college at York.

There was a great deal of prejudice against McPherson's ideal of a college-trained ministry in the Methodist church in mid-Victorian times. Preachers like John Oxtoby, who had converted the fishermen of Filey, called prepared sermons "paper pellets". He preferred to know only his text when he stood in the pulpit. The rest he left to the Spirit.

They were singing that old Methodist hymn "We shall overcome" when Stephen Blakeston mounted the steps to the pulpit. He sat with his head bowed in prayer until the singing ended. Whatever the Methodists might lack, it was not joy in music-making. The society at Norton were proud of their choir, and not without reason.

Someone said of Stephen that "when he goes up t'steps into t'pulpit he looks quite ordinary. When he starts a-preaching, it's like he's somebody else."

All his diffidence and his unassuming, rather colourless personality disappeared as soon as he stood and faced his hearers. It was replaced by a figure of authority, as if he had donned some priestly robe. The effect was all the more powerful because his power over his hearers came from something invisible.

He spoke quietly and without the extravagant gestures of the old-fashioned Ranter preachers. He did not ask at the end of every sentence: "Are you saved?" "Have you found Jesus?", but his words, like his eyes looking steadily at their faces, searched the souls of his hearers and humbled them.

He had chosen as his text the verses from St. Luke on the Good Samaritan.

What a terrible temptation it must have been for that Samaritan to pass by, as the priest and the Levite had. How many in his congregation, had they lived in those days, with no police force, no means of knowing when the thieves might return, how many would have gone by as quickly as possible?

Excusing themselves perhaps, as they hastened on their way, by thinking that probably the man had brought trouble on himself by being in bad company - a drunken brawl, perhaps - wasn't there an inn nearby? Whatever had happened, after all, it was none of their business. How many, seeing someone in trouble or disgrace, someone they had never met before, with whom they had no ties of kinship, would say: "I don't want to get involved" - as if that was the way of virtue?

He reminded them that, in the Garden of Gethsemane, Christ Himself had known what it was to be left alone with his grief. "Would ye not watch with Me one hour?" He asked the disciples. But the disciples who loved Him had slept during the hour when He most needed them.

And yet, Stephen added, when there was trouble in a family, how many people could find time to gather with their neighbours - not to try and find some way of helping the family through their hour of trial, but to gossip and condemn, even, in that way which is part of fallen human nature, even to enjoy the downfall of another.

"Have you never seen them gathering at street corners or by the well, ready to point a finger, their tongues all too ready to tell the tale of someone else's sin. Like carrion crows, looking for whatever is rotten and relishing it! Isn't that what a gossip does?

"Do you never stop to think how some poor fallen woman, like the girl Hetty in 'Adam Bede' who murdered her own child, might have been driven to insanity by the lack of loving care at a time of great need? Driven by all those people who shut their doors and their hearts when they saw a poor, homeless girl with a baby in her arms, the people who said: 'We don't want to get involved'. Weren't they the real murderers, the ones who were responsible for the death of the child, and not the wretched girl-mother, half-crazed with fear and starvation?"

He reminded them that the woman preacher Dinah Morris, who accompanied Hetty to the scaffold, was really Mrs. Mary Evans, the wife of Samuel Evans, the brother of the novelist, and a Primitive Methodist.

"Let us be proud and thankful that Mrs. Evans in real life did this deed of mercy for another unfortunate young woman. We know that, whatever her sins, going to her death with such a true Christian beside her, that young woman must have found repentance and the forgiveness of the Lord in her last moments."

Stephen reminded them of the hymn they had just sung, and of the victory of Lincoln at Gettysburg that summer. "How many rich planters and their families, surrounded by every luxury and refinement, had shut their eyes to the evils of slavery. How easy it was if your own life was free from trouble to turn aside form the sufferings of others, or to judge them harshly – even to think, as some did, that poverty and distress were always the result of idleness and lack of thrift. We all know how difficult life can be, however hard they try, for some. Instead of gossiping about their troubles and temptations, let us go to their help if we can, if only to listen to their sorrows, but let us go quietly and humbly, not in order to be seen of man as the Pharisees did, but as if we truly believed that we are all members of one another in Christ.... Amen."

When he had finished speaking, in the short silence before the rustling of pages and the coughs that had been suppressed or forgotten while he was preaching, Martha had the strange, irreverent thought that this young man, who had held them spellbound by some quality which existed apart from his words, though it helped to lend them significance, should really be rewarded by a storm of clapping, instead of the ejaculations of "Hallelujah!" and "Praise the Lord!" which soon followed.

Stephen was being entertained overnight at the house of Martha's distant cousin, Lilah. He had hoped to see Martha there after the meeting, but as usual Giles was waiting for her with the gig.

They had only met for a few minutes that day, but she must have made an impression on him, because it was not until a year later that Stephen was able to meet her after the meeting. It was Martinmas Day, 1864, when she was invited to supper at Lilah's with her Aunt Lizzie and Uncle Robert.

It was obvious to Lilah and her husband Martin Summers that Stephen was attracted to Martha. They were both anxious that this time the young people should have a chance to be alone together.

"Martha, my dear. I believe you haven't seen the new Bethel yet, have you? It's very nearly finished, you know. The painters start work next week."

The New Bethel had been the topic of Primitive Methodist conversation, of heated discussions, earnest prayers, letters to the Connexion, and a vast amount of unpaid work put in by Martin, who had the contract for all the woodwork. Of course he had to pay the two men who worked for him. Martin's business had expanded considerably since he was the village carpenter, making coffins and cupboards. So he was a good deal out of pocket when he had finished working on the pews - but what was the good in having wealth if you couldn't give it to the Lord?

The builder and the joiner were both Methodists, craftsmen who took a pride and joy in their work. The architect had come from Hull, and he had designed an edifice which exactly suited both the old-fashioned Primitive Methodists who were so afraid of any kind of ornament and the good taste of men like Martin who admired the eighteenth-century simplicity of design in the Georgian houses which were, in mid-Victorian times, not at all fashionable.

Martin enjoyed showing them the interior of the new chapel to be opened in a month's time. "Martha, my dear. I've just remembered old Samuel Jarvis is coming to see me about one of the items the committee queried. Stephen, here are the keys. Don't forget to observe the communion rail. I'm rather pleased with it. There now, I must be off. I'll see you later."

Martin's hand touched the smoothness of the oak, which had been turned on his own lathe. The architecture of the new Bethel might be plainer than the pseudo-Gothic tabernacle the Wesleyans had erected in 1858, but he knew that the craftsmanship of the interior was incomparably finer than theirs. The Wesleyans might have more money than the "Prims", who had had to wait until 1864 for their own place of worship in Norton, but the New Bethel was a building of which they could be proud.

Silently, in obedience to Martin's wish, Martha stood for a moment by the communion rail, with Stephen behind her. Facing the altar and the pulpit, she was perhaps more readily influenced by what he had to say to her than she would have been anywhere else.

Stephen was not particularly good-looking. He was pale and studious with mouse-coloured hair and spectacles; he had little physical charm, but when he preached he had held the attention of the congregation by an animation and force of personality which no-one seeing him elsewhere would have believed possible.

Even the older members of the congregation who did not hold with book-learning could not deny that Stephen "had the Spirit". He would go far in the Ministry, Martin had prophesied. He would be a great preacher one day.

So Martha, although she was not in love with Stephen, was flattered and troubled when he took her hand and told her how long it had seemed since he first saw her and how much he had looked forward to seeing her again.

"You know, Martha, we shall probably have to wait a long time before we can meet again, though I pray that the trustees here may decide to invite me once more."

He paused. It was not for him to say that he felt his sermon that night had been very well received, even though he had been warmly congratulated on all sides.

"Thay are going to do that, Stephen. I heard Mr. Sumners telling his wife you was going to be invited to preach at the opening of the New Bethel. That's how much they thought of your sermon, Stephen. It was wonderful. Martin says you will become a great preacher and do great things for Methodism."

"He is too kind, Martha. But I do believe God had called me to the ministry. I do mean to use whatever powers He has given me in His service, to win souls." His hand was upon hers now.

"Martha, I feel as sure as I did when I heard the call to be a minister that He has chosen you to be my helpmeet. I know you would make a wonderful wife for a minister, Martha, and I would do everything I could to make you

82

happy. Will you think about me, at least, when I am away? And will you promise to write to me?"

To have an "understanding" with a student for the Methodist Ministry was something that would make her the envy of most of the other young women in the congregation. All the influences of her home and her religion combined to make her feel it was a great honour that he should have chosen her, and the fact that they would see each other at long intervals, that they could not dream of marriage until he had passed his examinations and completed a year's probation in the ministry - all this made it seem at that moment that perhaps it wasn't impossible for her to enjoy the friendship of such a young man. Instinctively, Martha knew that Stephen was as inexperienced sexually as she had once been.

She was still under the spell he had cast when she had heard him preaching from the pulpit, not in the least like the shy, earnest, but very determined young man who was pleading with her now. When he took her hand she could not withdraw it, but she could, or rather she must, say something that would make him understand that after all she could never be destined to marry anyone, and that she certainly could never be a minister's wife.

"I ... I don't think I'm the right one for you, Stephen. You ought to look higher than a girl like me."

"I'm as sure that you are right for me as I was sure when God called me to the ministry. I don't want anyone else but you, Martha. I know God has brought us together."

He spoke quietly, but with such absolute conviction and sincerity that Martha almost felt convinced herself that somehow or other she was destined to be his wife. And then, that day would be so far off. Before they went back to the others, Martha had promised that she would receive his letters and write to him. Someday in the future they would be engaged and then married. For the present they had an "understanding".

Martha wept that night, although it was Martinmas and she was at home, sleeping with Tilly and one of the little ones. She could not sleep three in a bed, and the cottage was stuffy. She longed to get up and sit by the open window, but she did not want to disturb her cousins. Tilly had a hard time of it now that Aunt Lizzie's health was failing. She should have been out in service like Martha, but she was needed at home. If Tilly had known that Martha had the chance of marrying a young man who was going to be a minister, how excited she would be.

Of course she would have to tell her family, but not that night. With Stephen's departure, his one kiss a failure, their noses getting in the way, proving to her that he had absolutely no knowledge of women, all her doubts, all her self-reproach and guilt came flooding back.

"How could I have let him think we can have an understanding. Misunderstanding more like." Poor Martha lay restless, weary but sleepless, wondering how she was going to tell Stephen the truth. Well, she had promised to write to him. That was the answer. After all, it would be easier to write than to tell him face to face what had happened. But she could not bear the thought of anyone knowing how Henry Marney had behaved on his last night in England. She could never tell Stephen anything that reflected on the family she loved so much.

When she heard anyone talking about Henry - and there had been plenty of talk after he left the bank - Martha always refused to say any more than that she hoped he was doing well and that she knew his mother missed him very much. People used to say: "It's no good pumping Martha, she jist clams hup if you hask 'er owt about t' Quakers". But a few of them admired her for her loyalty to the family at The Mount. Others of course were annoyed because she was not a gossip.

"Stuck up little madam, Martha Cousins is," they said. "Too strait-laced, that's her trouble. She dain't seem has if she's hinterested in anythink but singing 'ymns at Methody meetings. Tis a good thing she's got a place cos a lass that's been 'usband-'igh as long as she 'as and nivver walked out wi' a lad nivver will."

That was their neighbour Maggie Bilson, but she was prejudiced against the Ranters and always had been. Some said if her Amos had taken to joining the Ranters instead of his regular sessions at the King's Head, poor Maggie might have had an easier life and a less sharp tongue for her neighbours.

Stephen had told her in one of his letters, unnecessarily, that he had never held a girl in his arms. Of course he longed to hold her. He knew she would be pure when she came to him as his bride, and he assured her that God had given him the strength to keep him as spotless as she would be.

She went about her work at the Marneys with that shadow over her, her nerves worn by her sense of guilt and the conflict about telling Stephen. At night she was almost afraid to go to her room, to remember again all too vividly that night before Henry went away for ever.

His parents were ghosts of what they had been when she first came to that fine house which had seemed a paradise on earth, the home of an ideally happy family.

She must tell Stephen somehow, sometime, but after all she could not put it in a letter. They would not meet again until the opening of the New Bethell at Norton in November. She would tell him then, after he had preached, not before. There would be an extra large congregation, and important preachers from Hull who had promised to come. Of course it would mean the end of their "understanding", the end of that new dignity which had been hers in their little Methodist community, of being the one chosen by the brilliant Stephen Elvidge Blakeston.

Almost a generation earlier, it had become fashionable for Wesleyan Methodists to give their sons the middle name of Wesley. Outside the Wesleyan chapel at Norton, built in 1858, it was not uncommon to see the name of a visiting preacher, billed like an artist at a music hall as the star attraction of the programme:

10.30 and 6.30
THE REV. T. WESLEY FIELDING.

The "Prims", rejected originally by the Wesleyans because of their fondness for Camp Meetings, did not christen their sons "Wesley", but even with them the fashion for important-sounding middle names which would look well on the board outside the chapel had begun. Names like D. Paradine Frost were popular now among the Methodists, and obviously Stephen's parents had thought that if their son "heard the call" an impressive middle name would be no hindrance to his success.

Stephen's parents had a small bakehouse in Ardwick, then a very unsalubrious district of Manchester. They were poor and hard-working, and they kept themselves to themselves, as the neighbours said. Their ambition was to keep out of debt and if possible do well enough to move further from the city centre to the equally grimy but more genteel district of Longsight.

Stephen had one sister, Helen, and a younger brother Bernard Sackville, who wanted to be a carpenter. Bernard was the delicate one of the family, and he died of consumption when he was seventeen. It was a narrow home-life for them all, with their childhood bounded by the Sunday school and chapel three times on Sundays and prayer meetings during the week.

As well as being an unusually small family by the standards of their day, they were a very close-knit one. Too shy with outsiders, they did not form friendships easily, and in any case it was not the sort of home where you could ask your friends to drop in unexpectedly. Their mother was "particular", too particular about her house and about her family, always asking them where they had been, and with whom.

It was not easy growing up in such an atmosphere, and Stephen, studious, spectacled, withdrawn, did not have a happy adolescence. It was hard to think of his ever being able to mix easily with other people, ludicrous to suppose he could ever stand up to address a crowd.

But miracles happen sometimes. A minister of unusual intellectual ability and the gift of communicating his enthusiasm to others came to Joseph Street and stayed for six years. At the end of three years a Methodist minister had to wait for an invitation from his congregation to stay or was sent elsewhere by Conference.

He introduced Stephen to other young men who were going to college and he brought him to the notice of the Rev. John McPherson. Stephen had a good brain and could speak well, once he had conquered the almost crippling shyness which was born of the taboos of his home.

He had found the courage to answer "the call" which must come from God to every Methodist minister. By God's grace he had conquered that terrible sense of shame which had once made him incapable of saying a word in front of others.

It had been very good for him, the training for the ministry and the travelling away from home, preaching in chapels and houses in different parts of the district assigned to him by Conference, that annual gathering of the Methodists which was all-powerful in much the same way as the Trades Union Congress, which based a lot of its organisation upon that of the Methodist Conference.

Stephen had started early on the road to success in his chosen career. Through the influence of the Rev. John McPherson and through his own gift of preaching he had escaped from his restrictive home environment. He had found himself, and now, at the age of nineteen, he believed that in Martha he had found his mate.

Letter from Sarah Blakeston, July 3rd, 1864.

My Dear Stephen,

I can still hardly believe that my own son, the son we have sacrificed so much for so that he can answer God's call to the ministry, can write and tell me he has an understanding with a servant girl, not yet sixteen.

Oh my dear son, I have prayed all night on my knees to God to lead you back to the path He has chosen for you. I shall never stop praying for you.

As your mother, who has struggled harder than you can know to bring you up as a Christian and a gentleman, I pray and beseech you, don't

88

let yourself be dragged down into the mire by the desires of the flesh and the wiles of the Devil.

Your father has had bronchitis again and is far from well. I thought the shock of your letter would have killed him. He never complains that he has no son to help him in the bakehouse, only two weak women, when we can spare time from the house.

John, Ellen, Charity and Thomas Whitworth at Number 70 have all died of diptheria within a fortnight. They say Mrs. Whitworth can't pay the undertaker and if there is another death in the family it will have to be a pauper's grave. Thank God I have always managed to pay a shilling a week to the Burial Fund, though it has never been easy.

The Rochdale Pioneers are going to open another Co-operative just round the corner in Danzig Street. Your father is afraid it will take his profit, which is little enough as it is. But we have always found money somehow for your books and schooling. I know this won't be easy to read, Stephen. My tears are falling on the paper as I write. I hope you can read enough to make you realise what sorrow you are causing us.

Please God you will repent of this folly before it is too late and not let this hussy ruin your life and all our hopes for you.

You are still my son and I am praying for you.

Yours in Christ, Your sorrowing mother.

Letter from Stephen Blakeston, July 4th, 1864.

Dear Mother,

I am sorry indeed that you have judged so harshly the young woman I intend to marry. I can only tell you that when you know her you will realise how needless are all your fears.

Martha comes of a respectable Primitive Methodist family who are well thought of by all who know them. She is very highly esteemed by her employers, who, as I told you, are Quakers and who have been more than kind in welcoming me to their home.

I may add that the custom of girls going into service in big houses in this part of Yorkshire does have some advantages. If they marry, they do know how to run a home. Martha has a natural reserve of manner except when with her family, who love her very much, as they ought.

She dresses as plainly as is expected of a Primitive Methodist and is in every way fitted to become the wife of a minister one day, God willing.

I do not doubt that when Martinmas comes — that is the end of the servants' year - and I can bring her to see you, you will rejoice that God has sent me such a helpmeet.

Let not your heart be troubled, my dear mother. I am well in mind and body, but your letter made me very unhappy. If only I could make you and father understand that I feel as if the most wonderful thing in the world has happened to me. Surely it is not a sin to be in love? Cannot you believe, my dear mother, that I may have chosen as wisely as my own father did when he chose you?

Please, mother, try not to give way to that tendency you have to look too much on the black side. Try to believe God has sent me Martha and that you will come to love her one day as a daughter.

I thank you with all my heart for your prayers. Try to believe they have been answered, that your son has no desire to stray from the path God has called him to follow, that far from being dragged down I have been raised up and strengthened in my faith by my dear girl.

You know I would give my life to spare you from sorrow, my dear parents. I never forget for a moment all the sacrifices you have made for me.

Give my love to Helen and please, mother, do visit Mrs. Whitworth, even though she doesn't go to chapel. Tell her they are in my prayers. And if father can spare anything at all from the bakehouse, do let them have it. Remember it is our duty as Chistians to love one another.

Your loving son, Stephen.

CHAPTER NINE: MARTHA'S ILLNESS.

Martha was overworked more and more through Nanny's failing health. She sat up with her night after night, unknown to her employers. Poor Nanny didn't want anyone to know how ill she was, except Martha. Martha was good at keeping secrets.

Her own secret was the hardest to bear, and her own health began to suffer - a combination of sleepless nights and inner conflict was taking its toll. She had lost weight, and at a certain time after meals she hardly knew how to keep going at her work. She felt so weary, and the nagging pain in the middle of her stomach got so bad that sometimes it was excruciating.

One day, when she was helping Ellen to make the bed in Mr. and Mrs. Marney's room, she had a fit of coughing. She could not help herself, she vomited blood onto the spotless counterpane. She was too sick and faint and in too much pain even to care about what had happened. She had never been ill in her life until then, and she felt as if she was dying.

Dr. Arkwright was sent for. He prescribed complete rest and a very light diet, mainly milk and eggs. When he asked Martha about the pain, she said: "It only feels like something the size of a sixpence, Doctor".

"If you had a piece of bread and butter, Martha, which would you rather put on it, salt or sugar?"

"Salt," said Martha immediately.

"That's it!" cried the doctor, who had a reputation for being clever at diagnosis. "You are eating too many salty things. Cut them out!"

He told them that Martha had a stomach ulcer. She would have to go home and rest as much as she could. Mrs. Marney assured her

that when she was better she should come back to
them. "I don't know how we're going to manage
without you, Martha."

On some women's lips, those words might
have sounded like a rebuke. It was really so
tiresome for a servant to be ill. But Martha's
mistress spoke gently: she knew how she would
miss Martha's presence in the household.

Mrs. Marney was pale and drawn. She was
worried about the news of an outbreak of typhoid
in London. Gavin's letter had not arrived that
week, and every morning the lack of news from
Henry cast a shadow over the rest of the day.

Martha was driven home in the gig with a
parcel of groceries and her Martinmas wage, a
sovereign in advance. In addition, Dr.
Arkwright's fee for attending her when she was
at home would be paid by her employers.

Aunt Lizzie found Martha a difficult
patient. She would not rest as much as she was
told. But, after all, there was not the
exacting daily routine of a large household, and
the simpler food, a little often, as the doctor
advised, helped to heal the ulcer. She
recovered completely in less than two months,
and her digestion never troubled her again.

But it is known today that such things are
caused not only by too much responsibility, too
much rushing about, but also by secret fears and
worries - "stress", to use a word that is more
overworked than any Victorian skivvy.

Being at home, Martha was free to go to the
meeting on Sundays. This was a great joy to
her, and it was soon obvious to others -
although Martha never talked about their
"understanding" - that Stephen had fallen in
love with her.

Aunt Lizzie was pleased for Martha. Nobody
could wish for a better husband for a favourite
niece than a young man who was going in for the

ministry. She was surprised that Martha was so very reserved with him, hardly raising her eyes to him and seeming to avoid him whenever possible.

It was not often that Martha and her aunt were alone in the cottage, but perhaps Aunt Lizzie had arranged it somehow. Only two of the youngest children were near when she decided it was time to tackle Martha about Stephen.

"You can't help knowing he likes you, and he's always asked after you when you was at The Mount, and now when you go he's dying to have a bit o' talk wi' ye. Ivverybody can see it. Ye couldn't wish for a nicer young man. There's no need to act like you diz, Martha. I declare, I was that sorry for him last Sunday I could have cried. You know he has to stay in Manchester while he's taking them exams. Well, I expect by the time he comes again he'll have found a nice young lady in Manchester, and I'm sure I wish him well. But I wish I knew what you'd got against him, I wish I did. Lilah said to me, she says: 'I'm so glad Stephen Blakeston's hinterested hin Martha. She would make a very good wife for a minister,' that's what Lilah said. Now what can ye have against him, Martha love, or is there somebody else?"

Martha simply could not answer. She and Aunt Lizzie had always been so close. She had never kept anything from her aunt but this one thing.

"Can't you say something, Martha?" Her aunt spoke a little sharply. Martha was forced to turn her face from the fire, and Aunt Lizzie saw the tears running down her cheeks. In a minute she held her in her arms, and Martha was sobbing that she would never be able to marry anybody. She could never be a minister's wife, or anyone's wife.

"It was Mr. Henry. I never let him touch

94

me before, but when he came to me that night – it was the last night before he went to Australia – he didn't want to go. He was terrified of going so far away. He came to my room, and he said he'd shoot himself if I didn't let him in. He said he couldn't stand being alone that night. I was sorry for him then, but I know now what a fool I was. Oh God, what I've been through! What I've been through!"

Aunt Lizzie was shocked, but it did not occur to her to doubt Martha's word. As a child she had got into trouble sometimes for telling the truth at inopportune moments, but, as Uncle Robert had said once, it was better to be like that than to be too ready with a lie.

"Hush, love. It's all over now. My poor bairn. Ye ought to have told me, love. Ye see, love," Aunt Lizzie's mind was busily at work. She was as guileless as Martha, except when it came to schemes for her loved ones. "Ye see, love, though it was a bad thing, ye wain't so much to blame, and it seems to me as if ye've been punished enough. You're a good girl, Martha. If ye wain't it wouldn't have been such a trouble to ye. Now just stop crying and listen to me."

Aunt Lizzie paused. She was remembering the time when Stephen had "given them a glister", that sermon which had been based on the parable of the Good Samaritan. He had spoken out then about gossips who condemned when they should have held their tongues and gone to help. Surely, of all men, Stephen Blakeston would be the last to turn against a poor girl who had been betrayed as Martha had been? And yet, he was in love, and he was a man, albeit – when he came down from the pulpit – such an extremely shy, silent, young man. In spite of all his book-learning, in spite of his wonderful gift of preaching, she was sure he was as

95

innocent as Martha had been.

It wasn't only girls who could be ignorant about the facts of life. Wasn't it even possible that Stephen, himself a virgin, knowing so much about books and the Spirit and so very little about ... all that, wasn't it even possible he might be deceived on his wedding night?

She whispered to Martha: "If ye was to tell him 'twas all an old wives' tale 'bout bleeding and that, why, he wouldn't know any better, maybe. I've heard o' stranger things than that. Besides, love, even if you was to tell him the truth when you was his wife, he'd know it wain't your fault. He'd believe ye, love, same as I do. You're a good girl, and it can't be wrong for ye to get a good husband since God's sent ye one like Stephen."

CHAPTER TEN: JANE.

It is not strictly true to say that Martha and Ben met for the first time when they were introduced to each other by Lilah at the opening of the New Bethel in Norton in December, 1864. They had seen each other briefly at Townsend's shop when she was sent there once by Mrs. Barr with an order for the Marney household.

Going into that well-maintained establishment with its black and white marble floor, shining mahogany counters, high-backed bentwood chairs which were completely hidden by the customers' crinolines when they sat down, the maid-of-all-work from The Mount had been almost afraid to look around her.

She had gone to the furthest counter where there were one or two more modestly dressed customers, and she had been impressed by her first sight of Ben, who came forward to serve her, because he was such a very good-looking youth. He had the fair hair and blue eyes she had admired ever since she had met Gavin Marney, and Martha was also impressed that Ben was so perfectly self-possessed and at ease in what to her were the rather grand surroundings of Townsend's.

It did not occur to her that in her own place of work, in one of the finest houses in Malton, helping to run the home of a rich banker's wife, she herself never felt shy with the family for whom she worked. Here in these strange surroundings she was unusually timid.

Ben went out of his way to put her at ease. His observant blue eyes had noticed her as soon as she came in. He admired her neat figure and the sheen of her black hair, and when she raised her eyes he thought how lovely they were. She was plainly dressed, and her hair was not curled. She looked like a Quaker or a

Methodist, but he thought that perhaps she was not as prim as she looked - he noted the generous curve of her mouth.

"Please, do you have a dozen of the best wax candles, and do ye have soap made with oatmeal, and one with witch-hazel." Only the well-to-do households bought such items as soap and candles at Townsend's: ordinary people made their own. Then there was the pound of freshly roasted Kenya coffee. The housekeeper had sent Martha on a Thursday, because it was on Tuesdays and Thursdays that the coffee beans were roasted at Townsend's. The delicious aroma was all part of the atmosphere of luxurious abundance in this wonderful shop. Only the family drank coffee after dinner. It was not permitted in the kitchen.

Very carefully Martha put the coffee beans in a separate basket from the soap and candles, which had been expertly wrapped by Ben. He also weighed four pounds of currants and four of sultanas and then three ounces of yeast. Before they parted at their first meeting, Ben said civilly: "I hope I see you again, Miss".

Luckily, Ben's boss was at the other end of the shop, and Martha, blushing slightly, told him her name. She knew that he was called Benjamin because she heard a lady ask for him as she was going out of the shop - a very pretty, exquisitely dressed lady with a lilac parasol which matched her crinoline and a fashionable bonnet.

Martha held her head higher as she walked out of the shop with her purchases, but the surge of happiness a young girl always feels when she knows she is attractive - and to such a fine young man as that smart assistant at Townsend's too! - vanished abruptly the moment she stepped outside.

Drawn up at the kerb was a gig, with an

imperious-looking, dark-haired woman about to descend. Martha recognised Jane at once: she had not changed at all, thought Martha, but why should she have, when she had such an easy life?

Her brother John was handing her down. Martha stood rooted to the spot, transfixed as always by her mother's direct gaze. She opened her lips to speak, but Jane did not give any sign of recognition. Martha saw her brother blush deeply and heard him say her name. She flushed too, lowered her eyes, and turned to hurry down the street.

She felt within herself, in spite of her burning cheeks and the tears pricking her eyeballs, as cold and proud as Jane herself. After so many years of experiencing the selfless loving care of her Aunt Lizzie, after the courtesy and respect with which her kind employers invariably treated her, Martha's only coherent thought at that moment was: "What a mother! I hope I never see her again. She's not fit to be called my mother."

She turned as hurrying steps caught up with her. Her brother John, she could see, was deeply distressed and embarrassed. Martha looked at him with cool self-possession. "So, ye ain't ashamed of thi sister, John?" A tremor in her voice betrayed her feelings. John had once been her favourite brother.

He put his arms round her then and she remembered suddenly, as if it were yesterday, how he had given her a hug and a kiss when he left her at Aunt Lizzie's and she had wondered why.

"Martha, ye don't know how we've missed you. Ye don't know what it's like at home. You're better off where ye are, love. You know Mark's in Canada? He's got a farm of his own in Ontario. He wants me to go out to him, but I'm not sure. Ye see, he's getting married soon,

99

and I've seen enough of farms with too many to support."

"Don't go, John. Stay here. Why don't ye try and get something else to do? Don't stay and be a drudge for him and - that one."

"I know, Martha. That's what I'm trying to do. I'll have to go, she'll be looking for me. Ye see, love, she's got short-sighted. She didn't know ye. She can't see anything, hardly, without her glasses, and she won't wear them 'cept at home. I'm glad you're looking so well, Martha. You've grown into a bonny young woman. Are ye happy at your place?"

"Yes, I am, very. I hope ye find something, John."

Martha did not believe that her mother hadn't known her. She thought John was trying to save her from being hurt, as he used to when she was a child.

Ezra Townsend, who was serving Martha's mother, knew very well how bad her eyesight was. He had made the mistake once of indicating some jars on one of the shelves and asking which brand she preferred.

"Goodness gracious, man," she had said. "Do ye expect me to see from here?"

Ben knew Mrs. Jemison only as one of the customers who demanded to be served by Ezra. She had been labelled by the assistants as "poor, but mighty proud - a real tartar". They did not grudge Ezra the privilege of serving her.

Sometimes the lace which was used lavishly to trim her dark silk dresses was not as clean as it should have been. Her pale leather boots were often in need of polish, and her neat, well-fitting gloves had started to come apart at the seams.

There was no Annie at her beck and call nowadays. Annie was having a marvellous time, travelling to Egypt and Biarritz and the South of France with her employer, the wealthy Miss Melanie Jones, whose delicate constitution could not endure the winters in Yorkshire.

Jane, of course, was always treated with the greatest respect by Ezra Townsend, even when she was a very long time settling her account. Ezra knew a lady when he met one, but the younger end at Townsend's smiled at her eccentricities – her increasing shabbiness, her bad temper, and her habit of peering near-sightedly at the goods on the counter – only ever admitting that she was short-sighted when presented with a long overdue account:

"Oh, la, Mr. Townsend. Now I really can't see anything without my glasses you know, and I declare if I haven't left them at home again."

Martha, knowing nothing of this, distrusting Jane as she had always done, hardened her heart against her mother.

Jane was not even invited to Martha's wedding eight years later at St. Mary's in Old Malton, and the wedding announcement in the "Malton Gazette" gave Martha's name and address as "Miss Martha Cousins, of Old Malton". Very few people knew that Martha had any connection with Jane Jemison of Norton.

Her brother John would one day be employed by the firm of Ben Smith and Sons of Hull.

CHAPTER ELEVEN: MOMENT OF TRUTH.

Gavin Marney had nearly died of cholera in London. He had come home to convalesce, and finally it had been decided that he should remain at The Mount and take Henry's place at the bank. Somehow, now that the eldest son was at home, the shadow that had fallen on the family had lifted. Martha, as well as Gavin's parents and his brothers and sisters, felt much happier because he was at The Mount.

It made Martha's heart swell with deep happiness when he spoke to her about Stephen after they had been introduced.

"You know, I think, Martha, how much my mother values you. I think she was almost as anxious to meet Stephen as she would be if Emma told her she had met someone she wished to marry! Of course, we know it can't take place for a long time, but when we do lose you, Martha, we shall be consoled by the thought of your marrying such a fine man. Stephen will do very well. You will be proud of him one day, I'm sure, Martha, and you will be worthy of him."

Martha realised that, although in the eyes of her relations she was moving into a sphere of gentility and respectability worlds removed from the animal-like existence of the farm labourers, she would need all the home-making skills she had acquired at The Mount and all her inherited Yorkshire thrift and love of hard work to make ends meet as a minister's wife.

It was true that they would have a home provided for them wherever they were sent, but she did not think she would care very much for moving to a different part of the country every three years. It was almost a gypsy-like existence for Methodist ministers, compared to the comfortable vicar's life of a Church of

England clergyman with a good living.

Stephen's kisses were not quite so clumsy now, but even when he held her in his arms under the friendly, sheltering leaves in the lane where Gertrude and her gypsy lover had once abandoned themselves so recklessly, he never attempted any greater intimacy than a lingering kiss on her mouth - and sometimes it seemed to Martha that he was the first to break away.

"He thinks I'm made of glass," Martha thought, half-pleased, half-piqued. He wasn't usually the first to suggest sitting in the shade of the trees. He really seemed happiest when they were just walking together hand in hand, or with her arm in his, while he talked to her of his dreams and aspirations for a better life, not only for themselves, but for mankind as a whole.

Of course, her cousin Tilly had been greatly impressed by Stephen when she heard him preach. She turned and looked at Martha with envious eyes, as the other women did. What a wonderful life she would have one day, for sure, with such a man. Fancy our Martha marrying a minister!

But "off-stage", as it were, Tilly found her sister's young man heavy-going. "He's a lovely man, our Martha, and he's jist right for ye, Stephen is, but - well, I'm not jealous now, though I was at first. He - well - after all, he be a parson, bain't 'e?"

Sometimes, when he was hesitating for a word on their walks back to The Mount, Martha would supply some North Riding expression, to see his face change. It annoyed him so much when she did that! There were times when she could have bitten her tongue off for saying something in dialect, but she couldn't help herself. There was something within her that longed to bring him down to earth, just for a little while.

"Ye dain't like my jokes, do ye Stephen?"
She said it in a voice that was more thoughtful,
almost regretful, than he considered necessary.

He frowned. "I wish you wouldn't say
'dain't', Martha. It doesn't become you. You
don't talk like that with the Marneys and ...
you ought to respect me as much as your
employers. I don't want my wife to talk like a
servant. You see, Martha, I love you because
... because I can look up to you."

She remained silent as he continued: "I
see in you everything that is noble and good in
womanhood. I loved you when I first saw you.
You were so quiet and shy with everyone - except
your own family. I saw how you loved them, how
they loved you. I'll never forget that moment
at the meeting at Norton. It came to me in a
flash. I knew then that you were the girl I was
going to marry. It was like a revelation,
Martha. It was God who chose you for me, I
know."

Martha had heard these words before. It
disturbed her, this almost Biblical picture of
her, as if she had been selected as a fellow
saint to accompany Stephen in his calling. She
could not go on living a lie with a man as good
as Stephen, a man who idolised her, who could
not see her as she was.

"Stephen ...," her voice sounded strange to
her. "I have something to tell you - something
I should have told you a long time ago. I tried
to, when I said I was not good enough for you,
but I blame myself now for not being more honest
with you. I can't marry you, Stephen ... I'm
not a virgin."

Stephen was always pale, but suddenly now
he was ashen. He looked at her with those
searching eyes which so often had made his
congregation at once afraid, humbled, and

104

strangely excited. It was a look which she would never forget. She had expected him to question her, and she had decided that she would not tell him who it was unless he insisted, but - to her amazement - he did not speak. After that long look which struck terror in his heart, he sank on his knees and covered his face with his hands.

In that dreadful moment before he covered his face with his hands, Martha had seen his features contorted with shock, horror - and disgust.

All the taboos and terror of sex instilled in his early years by his neurotic mother took their revenge on him at that moment. Martha, despite her quiet, reserved manner and her Methodist plainness of dress, had been no different from the other village girls, no better than her cousin Tilly, who flirted with every lad she met in the street, whose behaviour had caused Martha such pain.

"It wasn't all my fault, Stephen. It ... it only happened once."

"I don't want to hear the details, Martha."

Stephen knew, if only from his reading, that a girl could be the victim of a man's lust without being a wanton, but although he had compassion for such unfortunates, he had no intention of marrying one of them. The lady of the Manse, like Caesar's wife, must herself be of stainless virtue, beyond reproach.

Martha was frightened by what she had seen in his face. She knew that he loathed her now as much as he had loved her - if it had been love. In the midst of her misery, there was that part of her that loved truth whatever the consequences, and it helped her now in that hour of humiliation. She knew that Stephen, with his idealism, his fear of physical contact, his lack of humour, might be a saint, but as a man he was

105

flawed.

She was not sorry that she had spoken, although his rejection hurt her pride. She was shocked, but she knew even then that she would get over it. It was for the best.

It was, after all, Stephen who suffered most. He had been deeply in love with Martha - or with that Madonna-like perfect woman of his dreams. He wept that night, when he was alone in his lodgings, before he wrote a letter to his mother.

A week later, when he arrived home, he was received by his mother and sister with unconcealed joy and relief, as if he had escaped some dreadful epidemic.

When he became a minister, his sister Helen kept the Manse for him. He would never fall in love again, although there were always women in his congregation who were ready to die for him - but his sister, who also never married, was very good at keeping them at bay.

Stephen became one of Methodism's greatest preachers. The City Temple at Westminster was filled whenever the name of the Rev. S. Elvidge Blakeston was outside, as that name filled every hall and chapel in the land.

The Methodists were always happy if they could get him to preach at the opening of a new chapel or an anniversary service. Stephen could always draw the crowds, and hold them spellbound. The Spirit never left him.

CHAPTER TWELVE: DEATH.

In 1865, when she had had the "understanding" with Stephen for just over a year, when Stephen was twenty and Ben and Martha were both sixteen, Martha was only just becoming aware that Ben not only admired her, but was determined to win her. Ben and Martha did not walk back to The Mount from Norton together until one Sunday evening in December 1866, but he had managed before then to be in her company at various meetings and love-feasts at the New Bethel. He helped with some correspondence for an appeal for a new harmonium, and Martha saw an envelope he had addressed.

"What a beautiful copperplate handwriting!" she exclaimed. "Where did you learn that?"

"At the Quaker adult school. I go there three nights a week. I'm learning book-keeping as well."

Martha liked Ben because he seemed so much more alive than anyone else she knew, and he found out that she enjoyed hearing about his childhood on the farm. He could make her laugh describing some character or incident that belonged to that period of his life.

"I bet he's had some sweethearts, that one, on the farm and in Malton," she thought, for she had seen him with one or two, "but 'tis a different thing for a man, 'tis only girls that's ruined for life."

Musing like this one day as she peeled potatoes in the kitchen at The Mount, Martha was startled by the sudden appearance of her young cousin Jamie, now seven and attending the village school. He had arrived at The Mount out of breath with running, his nose and eyes streaming because of the east wind - and he hadn't put his jacket on, silly boy. He had a smudge of ink on his nose and tears in his big, dark eyes.

"Goodness, Jamie, what a sight ye are! Whativver's to do?"

But she had known in her heart what it was even before he stammered: "It's me Mam. She wants ye - she's took ill." Jamie was very frightened, and was glad to hide his face in Martha's apron.

They were kind to him in the kitchen. He had a drink of milk and some biscuits, but he could hardly eat for the lump in his throat. Cook took him into the scullery and scrubbed his hands and face. The ink stains were a day old, for he had not been to school that morning and Tilly had been too busy to wash him. So by the time his cousin was ready and Giles had the gig waiting "at least he dain't look so lost and unbegotten," said Cook. She didn't want Martha to feel ashamed of him, but Martha had no eyes for poor Jamie that day.

She could only see Aunt Lizzie in her mind's eye as they neared the cottage in Norton. How frail she had looked last Sunday, how bad that pain must be when she had to sit down, whatever she was doing, and her lips went blue and she could hardly get her breath. "She was took bad in the night," Jamie had told her.

Her aunt was lying on the bed, well propped up with pillows, the patchwork quilt Martha had given her for a Christmas present over her, because they were waiting for the doctor. Martha could hear the effort of her breathing as soon as she entered the room. Aunt Lizzie's face was pale and had a sharp-featured look she had never seen before.

But her eyes, turned expectantly to the door, were bright with the joy of seeing Martha. She had come in time.

"Have ye any pain, Aunt?"

"No, love. Just the difficulty in

108

breathing." Aunt Lizzie's tone was patient and uncomplaining as always.

Martha sat holding her hand. Tilly was downstairs keeping an eye on the younger children, making some tea for Martha. Uncle Robert had gone for the doctor. Martha saw her aunt's eyes look wistfully at the window. It was open at the top, so that to Martha the room felt draughty. Did she want it closed?

"No, no, love. It's the air I want."

Martha opened the window wider and pulled the shawl more closely around her aunt's shoulders. "Do ye want me to read to ye, aunt?"

There was a Bible by the bed. Martha opened it and read "The Lord is my shepherd, I shall not want". It had always been Aunt Lizzie's favourite psalm. She closed her eyes as she listened. When Martha had finished, her aunt looked at her gratefully. She seemed to breathe, Martha thought, just a little easier.

"Come near me, love. Ye'll do all ye can to help him, wain't ye, and Tilly. She's not as steady as ye were, Martha, but she's a good lass. I hopes she gets a good husband - but not yet awhile. Keep an eye on her, wain't ye? And Martha, love, it's Ben you're going to have, bain't it? Ay .. Ah knew it was. He's a good lad. But Martha, ye must promise me ... ye'll tell him - about yer trouble. It's better he knows. Promise me."

"I'm going to, aunt. I dain't want no secrets. I'm going to tell him."

Martha stayed with Aunt Lizzie through that long day, that long, dreadful day that was still too short, because it was her aunt's last day on earth, and they had always been close.

The doctor came and went. He could not hold out any hope. There was nothing he could do.

Martha, her two eldest cousins, Walter and

Mark, and Tilly, were all kneeling in the room when Aunt Lizzie died in her husband's arms at half past seven in the evening of November 22nd, the day before Martinmas 1866.

CHAPTER THIRTEEN: BEN.

Perhaps Martha waited so long to tell Ben, in spite of that death-bed promise, because she wanted to be sure of her man. Ben had often talked of the tragic fate of his sister, Lily, who had been abandoned by her lover when she was pregnant, and never once had he said a word of reproach about what Lily had done. He had even, Martha remembered, told her that he did not think any the worse of a girl who allowed her lover to have his way.

"So long as two people are in love and are going to get married, I can't see that it's a sin, Martha," he had said, but she had never let him go too far with her.

They were walking back from the New Bethel one Sunday evening early in November when she heard Ben say: "I can hardly believe it's Martinmas again in just over a fortnight, love."

She didn't answer, and Ben looked at her, a little puzzled because her expression was suddenly so sad.

"You're looking forward to it, aren't ye, sweetheart? A holiday will do ye good, and Mrs. Marney always gives ye a present besides your sovereign. My Aunt Appleby told me she'll take nothing from me this year. She says I can pay her back one day when I'm earning more.... What is it, love?"

It would be even worse than Martinmas last year, Martha was thinking. Aunt Lizzie dead, and Ben would surely soon be gone out of her life for ever. She could not go on being a coward any longer: she must tell him the truth.

As she drew away from Ben, a gust of wind made her shiver and brought a flurry of bright gold leaves cascading from the old elm, prodigal of its wealth as the Welfare State these two would never know.

There were no tears in her eyes, but as she stood before Ben under the trees in the lane at Norton, she felt as cold as death, she felt as if they had already parted for ever and gone their separate ways.

She would never have any more to do with men, she thought. Thank God she had the Marneys. It was her fate to be a servant all her life, and she knew she would find a great deal of satisfaction caring for those she loved at The Mount. But at that moment she only knew how much she loved Ben.

Stumblingly, painfully, she told her lover what she has told Aunt Lizzie. "... It's true what they say, his father sent him away, and he didn't want to go.... He said he'd shoot himself if I didn't let him in. He'd never touched me before, I wouldn't let him."

Ben was silent for what seemed an eternity to Martha. "My God! And they called him a gentleman!

Martha did not dare to look at him. She stood with her eyes cast down, looking older because she was stricken. She was very pale, and her smooth, dark hair was drawn back as severely as the Methodists liked to see their women. Her high-necked dark dress had the jet beads she always wore on the bodice. The dress fitted well, showing her high bosom and neat waist. The skirt was hooped beneath the petticoats because it was Sunday, and even servant girls, when not in the kitchen, wore hooped skirts.

Her face was stern and drawn as he had never seen it before, so that she was no longer pretty. But to Ben, seeing her suddenly looking more like a woman of twenty-seven than a girl of seventeen, she was beautiful.

In a flash of foresight, Ben saw her at that moment as the wife of the successful businessman he knew he would become, some day. Martha had courage, she had a regard for truth and honesty as strong as his own. He knew nothing would ever matter so long as they were together.

His words, when he took her in his arms, were as gentle as her aunt's had been: "My poor lamb .. my poor little girl." He felt how cold she was, but life was coming back to her as she realised Ben's anger was not for her, only for Mr. Henry, who had betrayed not only Martha, but the whole ethos of the society they lived in, that sacred tradition of trust between the gentlefolk and their servants.

It was not all sorrow that Sunday when she told Ben, after all. Holding her in his arms for their last embrace in the orchard at the back of The Mount, Ben drew back for a moment, smoothed her hair very tenderly with his hand and whispered in her ear: "After all, love, we'll be saved a bit of trouble on our honeymoon."

Giles the groom, on his way from the stables, heard something he had never heard before. Martha, the little Primitive Methodist kitchen maid who was such a quiet girl, was laughing hysterically in the arms of her young man.

"Ay well," he thought, "young Ben's a lively lad, not like that milk and water preacher-fellow she used to be walking out with. 'Appen she'll be getting married one o' these days, Ah shouldn't wonder."

Martha was a good girl, but she was not an angel. It was not until almost a year after Aunt Lizzie died, when she and Ben were both eighteen, that she told him about Mr. Henry - in spite of that death-bed promise.

On Sundays, when she was granted an extra hour by her considerate employers, she had so many things to do at the cottage at Norton.

Tilly, who should have been such a comfort to her father, had, of course, got herself into trouble. She was going to be married as soon as possible to Harry Barker, who was an apprentice at the butcher's.

Ten-year-old Liza had a hard time of it, trying to take her mother's place, but luckily she was as strong as Martha. And Martha would never forget how good her Quaker employers were at this time. There was always something left over for the Cousins family on baking days, and Emma Marney abandoned her embroidery to make hard-wearing breeches and pinafores for the children.

Martha was very much in love with Ben, in love as she had never been with Stephen. She liked to listen to all he had to tell her about his life at Townsend's, when they were walking back to The Mount.

"Mr. McKenzie, the traveller from Hull, said I had the right personality to be a traveller, he said I could earn 200 a year." Martha gasped at this. "But I don't want to be a traveller all my life. I shall have a shop of my own one day, Martha, but it won't be here in Malton, because my cousin Johnny Appleby's going to open a shop here soon, my aunt and uncle are renting one for him. I know he won't get on, he's too feckless, but dain't say to anyone I said that. If I started in a shop of my own in

Malton and Johnny should fail, my Aunt Appleby and Uncle John might blame me for taking his trade. It wouldn't do, d'ye see. They've been good to me. I dain't want no trouble between relatives if I can help it."

Martha agreed. It seemed unfair, but he was right. Ben's judgement was always right, but the right time for leaving Townsend's was not an easy decision, even for Ben. If he stayed for seven years and completed his apprenticeship, he would be paid five sovereigns a year. It was not worth waiting for that, he told Martha.

His Aunt Appleby, hearing Ben's praises so often from Townsend's customers, knowing Ben was called in for the ritual of tea-tasting, had dreams of her nephew being a favourite of old Ezra Townsend, who had no sons. Perhaps he would put him in charge of the warehouse - old Peter was failing, everybody said - and then make him a kind of under-manager in the shop. Nobody could imagine Ezra not being in supreme charge, but, after all, he was getting on. He needed someone who knew the business, someone he could trust absolutely, someone who could talk like a gentleman, as Ben could, and who could deal with travellers as well as customers.

Ezra trusted Ben, but Ben never trusted his employer's intentions, so he was not as surprised as some of the others when one day Ezra called him into his office and he met Phillip Larard for the first time.

He was a pudgy, pasty-faced, dark-haired young man in his 'twenties. His dark eyes were not bright and sparkling but somehow muddy like his skin. He certainly wasn't prepossessing. He had a smug self-satisfaction, a sort of animal-like wariness, and he was Ezra's nephew. His mother, Mrs. Townsend's sister, was a very autocratic old lady, a customer who was always hard to please and never said "Thank you".

"My nephew Phillip has a good head on him," Ezra told Ben. "He's coming into the business, and he's going to start in the warehouse, like thee did, eh?" But that was a joke. Ben saw the sly look that passed from uncle to nephew.

Phillip Larard did go into the warehouse, at first. It meant that old Peter had more manual work to do: sometimes he was alone to do all the weighing out and tidying up. Phillip was in Peter's office, and was in charge of the ledgers which had once been Peter's sole province.

What would happen to old Peter, after his lifetime of petty tyranny over the young apprentices in the warehouse, his life of slavery to Ezra? Ben had never liked Peter, but he saw now how the old man's bitterness and hatred of anyone young and promising had its roots in fear and insecurity. What could he hope for if he was ill or too old to work? How could he have saved on the wages Townsend paid?

"Ezra ought to pension him off!" someone said and laughed. The idea of Ezra Townsend paying his longest serving employee a pension was ridiculous. "Paying people to do nothing? If they don't save for their old age, that's not my fault."

What happened to old Peter was rather more dramatic and less humiliating than the workhouse he feared so much.

In January 1867, after three months of a winter even more severe than usual in North Yorkshire, with snow falling every day from Martinmas until the second week of the new year, the sudden thawing of snow on the Wolds and Moors flooded the lowlands between Thirsk and Malton, so that the water was four or five feet deep in the hollows, and Malton was cut off.

The Derwent, the river which separated

116

Malton from Norton, looked like an immense lake, several miles in length. The Malton to Scarborough road was impassable, and on both sides of the Pickering railway the land was three feet deep in water. But in those days nothing was ever impossible for those heroes, the British workmen of the nineteenth century.

"On Saturday night, 26th ult," reported the "Malton Mercury", "floods on the Malton and York and Malton and Scarborough railways, and the other three lines meeting at Malton, as far as Norton junction, were twelve inches above the railway, and the utmost difficulty was found in working the traffic."

To make sure that passengers would be safe, the railwaymen ran pilot-engines out of Malton, every train going east and west, in order to prove the line ... "apprehensions being felt that the great current might remove ballast. Floating timber too gave fears of disaster, men in boats were engaged in keeping it off the railways. For several miles below Malton, the line itself was covered, but the trains got through."

Although the Malton and Scarborough road was "impassable for miles", the Post messenger "managed to get through on horseback, but with difficulty".

When Johnny Appleby came from the market in the early hours of that Saturday, he was wildly excited, as the young and irresponsible always are by anything that turns ordinary life upside down. He had come home by the high road, he had climbed on banks and walls to escape the flood water. He had seen, in that red dawn, drowned cattle and sheep, all kinds of floating timber, uprooted trees, barrels, cases from the biscuit works, and tables and beds from cottages, driven along by the strong current.

"How will Ezra like this, eh, Ben? What

about his new warehouse now? There wain't be
much left in it that's any good - everything
near the Derwent's under water. The biscuit
works and the gas works, ay, and the millers -
they say the millers 'as never been stopped for
twenty years, but they be stopped now."

Ben was as silent and serious as Johnny was
high-spirited as he dressed and followed his
cousin, who carried a lantern and a long stick.
"There's men in boats, see. Some are trying to
keep timber off railway, and there's them that's
glad to take what they can."

Suddenly the water was up to their thighs.
They struggled against the current to higher
ground: fortunately they knew every inch of the
road from the top. They looked down on the lake
that had been the river Derwent, often hardly
more than a stream in summer. Ben looked across
at the bank of the river where the millers and
Ezra's warehouse stood.

"He thought it was such a bargain, didn't
he, Ben? Old Ezra never could resist a bargain,
and he thought he'd get rid of old Peter by
putting him in it. My, but there'll be some
sacks o' flour and bonemeal wain't be much good
after this. It's flooded everything this side
of the river. They say it's three feet deep in
the millers."

Ben wasn't listening. Rain was still
falling from a sullen sky, adding to the water
still pouring from the Moors as the snow melted.
He stared at the warehouse, but in that gloom he
couldn't be sure. Something made him take
command. "Can we go in your boat as far as that
bridge? It's life and death - there's somebody
in that building."

No-one attempted to argue with him, though
he had no way of proving what he said. He
doubted it himself. It was incredible, but he
had to be sure. Johnny stopped chattering and

got in beside him. There was a dead sheep in the boat.

Ben thought he had seen a white face at the window. No-one would have believed it possible in that pale morning light, with the rain still falling. But Ben's eyesight was exceptionally good.

They clambered onto the bridge and made their way, waist deep in water, to Ezra's warehouse, which had cost him nothing as it was in exchange for a debt. They couldn't open the door against that flood, but there was a window which they managed to open, with difficulty. And then they were in real danger, in the darkness of the warehouse, with crates and cases as heavy as themselves swirling in the flood water.

Ben had never been in this warehouse. It was old Peter's domain, where he had been banished now that he was just a tiresome old man. He had one lad to help him, and a brand new set of ledgers to treasure. But there was no partitioned office, only a sloping desk at one end where he stood to make his neat entries so methodically, a dewdrop dripping from his nose from time to time.

Ben swung the lantern and suddenly cried out to his cousin: "There he is! He's in the water." Peter was struggling like a madman. He couldn't swim, and he had lost his footing. Although there was only four feet of water, it was rising every second.

He fought savagely against all Ben's attempts to raise him. Perhaps he was half drowned or only half sane. There was a roar of water outside. Ben thought they would all be trapped and drowned if Peter didn't stop struggling. Then he saw the heavy ledger on the desk. He picked it up and brought it down on Peter's head. Stunned, his threshing arms relaxed at last.

Ben hoped he hadn't killed him, but the old man's wheezing, bronchitic breathing was the only sound except the rushing water.

"He'll die of pneumonia after this, ony road," said Johnny prophetically as they heaved him through the window. There were more men with boats. Johnny shouted and swung the lantern over their heads. They were seen and helped into one of the boats, with Peter lying like a sack of potatoes between them.

"Cousin Ben's saved old Peter's life. He would have us go to t' warehouse, he thought he saw him at window. We nearly lost him, he were half drowned, he were fighting like a wild boar, he wain't let go. Ben had to hit him on t' head to get him out."

"Hush, Johnny, dain't let's talk about it. I couldn't have gone without thee. I reckon I'd have slept through it all if thee hadn't come and wakened me at half past four."

What could have made old Peter get up and make his way to the warehouse, the new warehouse he hated in his heart, as soon as he knew there were floods in Malton? Just as teachers, not so long ago, were given instructions by the Education Committee, in case of fire, to make sure they got the registers out of the building first - the children came second - so old Peter had been willing to risk his life to preserve his sacred ledgers.

Not a lot of things made Ben blush, when he was eighteen, but his customers at Townsend's made, as he said, so much fuss about how he had saved old Peter's life that his fair skin fired up as his sister Lily's had done when she was a new maid at the Big House.

"People forget about how brave poor old Peter was, going all by himself that night," he murmured, though it took him all his time not to add "the silly old man". But he was very sorry for his old enemy. It was not likely that he was going to live very long, even if he survived the chill that had turned to pneumonia. He would never be able to work again.

"Better for him, really, if he died, I suppose," said his Aunt Appleby, who had been to see him and taken some broth. Peter lived alone with only a little pauper girl to run his errands and care for him when he was ill.

"He used to call poor Sally a workhouse brat, I've heard him," said one of the neighbours. "He wain't be calling her that much longer, happen."

Everybody agreed it was a mercy when he died - in his own home, though alone. If he had lived, the workhouse would have been his last refuge - unless Ezra was shamed into doing something for him. But Ezra seemed even less inclined to be humane to his employees now that his nephew had come into the business.

"Times are hard, Ben. Dost tha think tha's earned another sovereign, doing tha duty? If I paid thee more than t'other 'prentices, what would they think? Ye must wait two years and then we'll see, till ye've been apprenticed seven years, 'tis the law. We can't be paying 'prentice boys tradesmens's wages. World's topsy-turvey enough as 'tis."

He hadn't even given him a word of praise, though Ben didn't care about that. He knew it wasn't likely he'd give him a rise, but his Aunt Appleby had had so much to say about it that he had promised her he would ask Ezra.

The fate of old Peter, Townsend's longest serving employee, made Ben lose respect for his tight-fisted employer.

When he got home, he wrote a letter in his best copperplate handwriting to Mr. Laverack, the chemist, who also sold a great deal of agricultural materials. He was familiar at least with some of his stock, and the traveller, Dan McKenzie, had told him that Laverack needed someone with brains who could be trusted with a bit of responsibility.

Over the years, he and Ben had been able to have enough conversation, while he was waiting for Ezra, for the older man to form a fair appraisal of young Ben's character, and then, of course, McKenzie had Scottish blood. Some people said he was "fey". He undoubtedly was a shrewd judge of character, and he had marked Ben out as easily the most able of the assistants at Townsend's.

"You're a Primitive Methodist, aren't ye, Ben? They're strong in Hull, and the Methodists aren't all poor people, not by any means. Some of them are doing well in business. That's what ye should aim at - a business of your own, in Hull. It'll come one day, mark my words. ... Ah, good morning Mr. Townsend. Benjamin was telling me how well that relish is selling."

While Ben was serving his usual customers, more popular than ever at Townsend's, and attending night-school, his cousin Johnny was enjoying himself with other free and easy spirits, a strange assortment of gentlemen farmers' sons and riff-raff, who were out shooting rabbits, rats, and moles, whose homes had been flooded.

Rats were seen even in trees, or perched on the railway lines as the water began to go down. It was capital sport, they said, the beating and shooting that followed after the floods. But the farmers of the lowlands had suffered great losses, not only from losing live-stock, but from the state of the wheat-lands, which would have to be sown afresh.

A few wreckers and looters were glad of whatever they could get from the swollen river, but the flooding of the millers, the biscuit works, and the gas works, as well as other warehouses like Townsend's, caused great hardship. Men were laid off because there was no regular work until repairs and rebuilding were done, and many died from starvation that winter, as well as from the usual epidemics.

Young children, shivering and coughing, huddling together for warmth in the damp cottages, died so fast that dreadful February of 1867 that it was said that the only people who prospered were the undertakers. There was never a day in Malton and Norton without at least one funeral passing down the street - sometimes with the black-plumed horses and top-hatted mutes, often, because the father was out of work and penniless, the corpse of a child carried simply on a bier.

Miraculously, the Cousins family survived. They had a dry stock of oatmeal in the loft, with apples carefully stored, but the soil was too heavy to grow the potatoes and turnips they usually had in their little plot.

Liza was quick enough at learning to take her mother's place, though it was a shame she couldn't have gone on at school, where she was doing so well, her father said. He wasn't one to take the sacrifices of his children for granted, but school pennies were not easy to find. The farmer who employed Uncle Robert had asked him to "wait a week or two" for his wage, because he had lost so many livestock in the flood.

Martha's uncle had no thought of marrying again, although, as Maggie Bilson said, when a Ranter lost his wife he had nowhere to go for companionship unless he started going to The Crown.

But he endured his loneliness somehow, talking to Liza, pleased to see Tilly, now big with child, and gladdest of all when Martha came.   And the Methodists were a caring people. Lilah and Martin Summers visited him every week, and Lilah always brought a packet of Townsend's best tea or a pie, and sometimes a ham.

CHAPTER FIFTEEN: THE COPPER KETTLE.

Martha's birthday was never forgotten by her employers, but in 1869, when she was twenty, she could not help wondering when Mrs. Marney sent for her that morning whether she had remembered the special significance of that date.

The Marneys were still at the breakfast table. Mr. Marney, Gavin, and Martin would be off to the bank in an hour. Young Edgar was there, his dark eyes sparkling as he looked at Martha. His little sister Rachel had been allowed down for breakfast, and Emma and Sarah smiled at her. Master Reginald was not present: he had left the Quaker school at York to go for a soldier, without his father's blessing.

Martha went in as demurely as if she was only expecting some message for Mrs. Barr, but as she glanced as usual at the hearth to make sure the fire she had lit hours earlier was burning well, she could hardly stop herself from giving an exclamation.

There, on a stand, was a copper kettle, a magnificent kettle, as fine as the one in the housekeeper's room.

Mrs. Marney rose and kissed her gently on the cheek. Her "Happy birthday, Martha dear!" was almost whispered. She seemed to be struggling with some deep emotion at that moment as she pressed her hand.

"You have served us well for seven years, Martha, my dear." Mr. Marney's hand was outstretched. "We thank you, Martha, and we all hope you will have very many happy returns of your birthday, and we hope that one day, when you use your kettle in your own home, you will think sometimes of your days with the Marney family."

Martha was glad the children were being naughty, quarrelling about who was to give her a kiss first. She felt as if she would never be able to speak.

"My dear Martha. I hope today will be happy for you, and that you will have many happy returns." Gavin's quiet, kind voice always had a calming effect on her. She gave him her hand gratefully. At last she could speak.

"It's so beautiful. I shall treasure it all my life. How can I thank you, Mrs. Marney? You are much too kind."

"Would you like it to stay on the hearth, my dear, till the day when you are married and have your own home? You must do whatever you wish. It is yours. You must think where you would like it."

Martha was kneeling by her lovely kettle, her hand caressing its smooth, shining surface. She looked up, with delighted eyes: "Please, Mrs. Marney, let it stay here, if you please."

"Now, my dear, will you ring for Mrs. Barr?"

Mrs. Barr entered almost immediately. She had been listening for that bell. "The other servants will be here in a moment, Ma'am."

They were just behind her, and now they filed in. Cook was at the head, followed by the two housemaids, Ellen and Kathleen, the new kitchen maid, Hannah, the nursemaid, Constance, who had taken over when poor Nanny died, Giles the groom, and the head gardener.

Mrs. Marney lifted the heavy kettle a little breathlessly and presented it to Martha. "This is a token of the value in which we hold our trusted servant, Martha Cousins, who has served this family faithfully for seven years. As you all know, today is also Martha's birthday. We all wish you a very happy birthday, Martha."

"Thank you very much indeed, Mrs. Marney, and Mr. Marney. I could not be happier than I am today. I only want to go on serving you as well as I can."

Martha could say no more. She heard Mr. Gavin say "God bless you, Martha!" as she returned the kettle to its stand on the hearth.

She was thankful to go quietly back to her duties. The little ceremony, which was such a historic moment in the life of a servant, was over. Every day now Martha would have her own copper kettle to polish in the breakfast room as well as the coal bucket, the fire irons, the brass fender and the warming pan.

Ben was doing well at Laveracks. He was entrused with collecting orders for the firm from farmers and from other shop-keepers. Somehow he always arrived looking as smart as he had done behind the counter at Townsend's.

His long legs, used to striding round the thirty-acre at Sledmere as a child, carried him from Malton to Driffield and back every Thursday, Market Day in Driffield, and sometimes he went even further than that in a day. He kept shoe-cleaning cloths in his pack of samples and never went to see a prospective customer without shining his boots.

He enjoyed the walk to Driffield over the top of the Wolds, from the North Riding with its stone cottages to the East Riding with the warm colours of brick and pantiles, where he always felt at home. He usually had a cup of tea in one of the cottages at Sledmere on his way back, when he brought them the news from Driffield and from Malton, and he heard there all the news of his friends.

He had plenty of time to plan his future with Martha as he walked across the Wolds. One day they would rent a little shop in Driffield with a room over it. He was getting to know so many people there, going on Market Days. He knew some of them would give him orders if he started in business there. He would specialise in tea. He would be a tea-dealer, not just an ordinary grocer.

He looked up Thomas Greenwood, the Methodist preacher they called "the little shoemaker" in Driffield. He took him his boots to repair - he had to keep them in good repair with all that walking - and he told Thomas how he had been converted by him at the love-feast at Tibthorpe in 1856, and how he had found the girl he was going to marry at another love-feast at the Bethel at Norton.

Martha was allowed a couple of hours off that June evening of mid-summer 1869 to go for a walk with Ben. Of course, they went to Norton, to see her family, so they didn't have a great deal of time alone.

Ben gave her a most unexpected present - something grander than she could have dreamed of - a length of black silk for a best dress. His Aunt Appleby had got it for him, and had said: "It'll make her think about marrying a fine young man and being able to dress like a lady sometimes 'stead o' slaving all her life at t' Quakers."

Ben was glad to hear about the copper kettle, and proud of Martha, and he liked Mr. and Mrs. Marney, but he thought she should have given the kettle to him, to keep at his Aunt Appleby's until they were married.

Why hadn't she taken possession of what was hers? It underlined something which worried him sometimes. Martha was too happy at The Mount, she was in no hurry to be married.

She tried to explain gently. "It seemed a good idea for it to stay there where I shall see it every day ... till ... till."

"Till ye get a family Bible to keep at the Marneys too? I'll tell ye, Martha, if ye think I'm going to wait another three years for thee, thou's making biggest mistake o' thee life! I've courted ye seven years, Martha, and I'm doing well enough now I'm travelling. This time next year, we're getting married."

They were married at last, six months after the Marneys had presented Martha with a beautiful family Bible, on December 16th, 1872, at St. Mary's Priory Church in Old Malton.

There was a family saying that my grandmother was so happy where she worked that she did not want to leave to get married, which she finally did when she was twenty-three.

It is as unlikely that a Primitive Methodist servant girl would wear a white wedding dress as that she ever had an engagement ring. Whether, two years after the crinoline went out of fashion everywhere else, it was still worn in the North Riding, I can't say. I would like to think that she wore a dress of dark silk with a hoop under her petticoats and the bodice trimmed with lace.

My mother remembered Martha saying that she was disgusted when she first saw someone wearing a skirt without a hoop. "It looked as if someone had thrown a bucket of water over them," was how she described the "new look" of 1870.

The "Malton Gazette" of 21st December 1872 carries their wedding announcement on the same page as the death of Lady Beaconsfield: "On the 16th inst. at the Parish Church, Old Malton, by the Rev. W.A. Rouse, Mr. Benjamin Smith of Driffield, to Miss Martha Cousins, of Old Malton."

Martha had been with the Quakers at The Mount in Old Malton for ten years. There can certainly be no doubt that from the moment she entered the Marney household on her thirteenth birthday, she felt, as a good servant did in those far-off days, that her home was with the family with whom she had found "a good place".

Martha's signature on the wedding certificate is more remarkable for an artistic hand than Ben's. Perhaps the church was cold and he was in a hurry to kiss his bride. He gave his occupation as "tea-dealer".

They were married on a Monday. On Tuesday they would both be busy in the little shop at Driffield, hard at work making their dreams come true.

It may have been possible in 1872 for Methodists to be married in their own chapels, but I am glad that Martha and Ben felt the need to have their wedding solemnised in the old Parish Church.

I have often thought, looking at the arched door of St. Mary's Priory Church in Malton that the marvellous carved patterns on the stone resemble the ripples in a pool, going on for ever.

Martha on her Silver Wedding